ALLIGATOR ZOO-PARK MAGIC

ALLIGATOR ZOO-PARK MAGIC

A NOVEL

C.H. HOOKS

BRIDGE EIGHT PRESS | JACKSONVILLE, FL

Cover art by Ty Williams
Book design by Cassie Deogracia
Published by Bridge Eight Press
Printed in the United States of America

ISBN: 978-1-732366-71-8
E-ISBN: 978-1-732366-72-5
LCCN: 2018966760

Special thanks to Matthew Logan for permission to reprint lyrics from "St. Francis."

For information about special discounts for bulk purchases, please contact Bridge Eight Press at specialsales@bridgeeight.com.

BRIDGE EIGHT PRESS
Jacksonville, FL
www.bridgeeight.com

For:
E, M, & B
&
M
&
Those we can't bring back.

*"They're all throwin' stones at the back of my home /
Kickin' the dirt in the air"*

— DELTA SPIRIT, "ST. FRANCIS"

PART 1

Jeffers - Master Magician

1

Jeffers was looking like a ghost hanging upside down from that big old oak tree, the one we used to swing from out into the spring's cool waters. That tree was there probably a few hundred years not thinking it would ever be used for magic. But there was Jeffers, his nice-guy eyes plugged deep, a sleight of spirit in a head full of hurt. He took in a lifetime of everybody's bad, and made good. He hung by his ankles—all slithered up in rope coils—a bunny wrapped-up in a snake.

"I don't get the trick," some city-boy was saying, still looking down to make sure they'd followed the right directions out into our woods and far out of feeling comfortable.

I don't know that anybody there was knowing what to make of Jeffers in the trees, rope creaking, hanging by his feet in the orangey-pink twilight. People were swatting at their bodies and listening to the crickets and the frogs get their songs started. That little sliver of a moon was peeking through the trees, winking at everybody like it was in on the joke.

There were probably about a few hundred people out in the woods—road leading there was lined with trucks, vans and big-tired trans, and folks were still walking up the road. They brought their beach chairs and picnic blankets. There sure wasn't enough space, so they just stood around eating buckets of chicken and drinking out of rolling coolers. I cut my nerves with some smoke and hustled through my first couple beers.

Jeffers cut me out. He cut his lady, Miriam, too. We tried asking separate, we tried asking together, but he just shook us off. I don't think he had a real reason other than the need to be alone. He wanted to go solo into the danger of this one, Miriam told me. The only people close to him, he blocked out. Instead, he got Judd. Didn't say why, wouldn't even talk about it, but it pissed me off plenty. Miriam tried to apologize for Jeffers, but didn't even know what to say about it. She didn't know a reason. Just knew I was hurt.

I stared over at Judd for a minute, and he felt me looking. Kept examining the rope in his hand, looking guilty and a little sheepish. I wanted to punch him in the lip, give him something to wipe on his shirtsleeve, to remember me by when I left for good.

Jeffers and me hadn't seen each other in over a week. It was the longest ever that I hadn't seen him since he ran off when we were just kids.

He'd been coming out here practicing for this trick. Wouldn't tell me where he was going when I called. I should've known when I told Miriam I was going swimming and she asked me to go pick her up some beer, instead. She knew I'd do it if she was buying— that I'd end up with some for myself. She never even drank beer. *Tricky, tricky.*

I looked up at the moon again. It wouldn't even shine enough light to let us see the trick. Don't know why we had to have the trick at the last of the light, but it was all on purpose. Jeffers didn't do these things for no reason. One deer-light off Judd's truck was pointed straight at Jeffers. Nothing else. It was still too warm for lightning bugs.

Some little hustler was walking around selling baggies like they were popcorn. "Shrooms! Shrooms?" Made me mad at first, then I bought some, pure outta hunger. Wasn't no need to get bent, things were weird enough. Even still, I popped a couple just to have something to chew on. Folks were always looking to make a buck. I was wondering if Jeffers was getting a cut—when Judd started in.

"Thanks for coming out everybody." Judd was tall—hunched and hairy—all loose jaws and tall gums. His sleeves were wet, maybe from wiping his mouth, and his shadow looked like it might lurk around in some kid's bad dream. "Ladies and gentlemens. Jeffers the Magnificent!"

Asshole waved his arm like a showgirl, then tried real hard to get that deer-spot right on Jeffers.

Jeffers looked wild and spooky, like he hadn't slept in a while.

"Tonight, I'm gone do the biggest trick you ever seen, yet!"

He didn't look himself. Maybe it was all the blood rushing to his head. Some folks started crowding in. I did too.

"These are some handcuffs from the sheriff!" Jeffers pointed down to Sheriff Chuck. He was eating out of one a them baggies. Taking a nice pinch in his fingers when Judd shined that spot on him. He looked up and smiled and finished the bite while he bobbed his head. Then gave a thumbs-up. Judd shined the light back on Jeffers.

"There's a whole bundle of gators down there." Jeffers motioned below. "They might be hungry!"

Judd moved, pointed the light down on the spring. Sure enough, there was a cluster of little shiny eyes. The light went back on Jeffers.

He got to tightening up the handcuffs and held his wrists out to the crowd. The handcuffs were real shiny. Looked like Miriam might've put some glitter paint on them. He showed us the keys to the cuffs, then dropped them in the water.

My buddy Tommy snuck up and nudged me. He whispered, "This shit for real?"

"I don't know." I was happy to start feeling the mushrooms. Knew I was answering honestly.

"Thought you always did?" Tommy was surprised. I was a little, too. "Always did before. You just ain't talking."

"Nope. I'm not in on this one." I pointed over at Judd with my thumb like I was hitching. "His new assistant."

"Huh." Tommy looked over there, his mouth hanging open and wheezing a mix of breath and whisky. "Weird."

Pete walked up and his brother Andy wasn't far behind rolling over another cooler. I was kinda relieved to see them. But there was definitely somebody missing. Miriam stayed home. Said she didn't want to see this one.

Judd hit a button on the tape deck and some techno circus music started pumping out in the crowd. City boys were laughing. Folks weren't taking it seriously, and I felt a little embarrassed for Jeffers. It took him a lot of years to get here. I was a little embarrassed for myself, too.

I heard another familiar voice. But it wasn't human. Wasn't no everyday gator. Sounded like a Cummins diesel wrapped up in gator skin. That bellowing was shaking water and rumbling and I knew then—things weren't right. *Lazarus* was out there in the water. Didn't know how he got there, but he was hungry for sure.

I swear Jeffers looked down at me. Nodded. When he did, that rope started getting longer. It slipped out faster and folks started freaking a little. I did too. Judd kept on giving him slack and lowering him down even when people started yelling *stop*!

Shadows of all the little gator logs crossed the water and I saw something big walking over top of all those little gators, just like it was walking on water. Lazarus was as big as a gator came and could jump out the water about the same as he was long. Sonofabitch looked like a dog going after a frisbee when he went to meet Jeffers at the end of that rope.

Jeffers gave out one last big moan and Lazarus gave about the same. They flopped in the water with who-on-top-of-who and splashed up a fountain back toward the trees. White cloth flattened on top of the water like a blanket, then made a sad sucking noise when it all got yanked under. For a second it seemed funny, then the whole world twirled around like smoke.

The sun gave out its last little bit of light and quit for the moon to take over for keeps. It didn't even get to set. A cloud covered it up and helped it slink away in secret.

Jeffers had never bullshitted me. He told me this one was going bad for sure. That thought didn't bring any comfort. Just made me feel queasy. I ran over toward the water.

"Judd, shine the light!"

Judd looked as sick and surprised as any, had this real blank face and got startled when I talked at him. He fumbled with the light and pointed it down on the water. All I saw was splashing and a bundle of little gators rearranging after all the excitement, and a stream of bubbles. It could have been the spring welling up or

Jeffers' last breath. I kneeled down on the bank and got the knees of my pants good and muddy trying to digest what I just saw. If Jeffers just got snatched up, there was a small chance he could make it back to the top—if he got the handcuffs off, if he could find which way was up, if he was still in one piece, if Lazarus decided to let him go.

The deer-light went out.

"Judd, keep the light over here!" I turned around and saw taillights where the spot-light had been. Judd was driving off. "Pete, get Chuck!"

But Sheriff Chuck was leaving too. Nobody wanted to wait around to be a witness. People were scrambling out into the woods, trying to get to their cars before the lines of traffic backed up. Everybody wanted to see Jeffers' big trick, but not a soul wanted to be a part of the fallout.

Me and Tommy and Pete and Andy split up on both sides of the bank and started walking down stream. We swatted bushes with sticks, shooing moccasins and small gators, knowing that if we came across Lazarus he'd probably be sleeping after such a meal. I found a boot, but it wasn't Jeffers'. Pete found nothing and Andy found a car battery. There was no doubting that Lazarus could've dragged Jeffers down in the caverns, no problem. A body could get hung up in there and never come out. But Lazarus would have to come up for air. Lazarus would've been a little more difficult to hide. I fully expected to have to cut him open and find pieces of Jeffers in his belly. Maybe his eyes would still be open, maybe he'd gasp out a last word, tell me what went wrong.

I heard Lazarus before I ever came up on him. Letting loose some big gator groans like he would when he got an upset stomach or kinda like Denny, my ex, when she was all knocked up. But this noise was a little different. I started thinking that maybe it wasn't Lazarus, but then I knew for sure when the moon lit up his markings and reflected off those eyes. They were pointed right at me, maybe twenty feet away and looking sad as could be.

"You sorry for what you done?" I started gurgling as soon as I started talking, probably sounding like I was drowning from all my snot and tears. Lazarus let out another one of those big guttural groans, then a snort. "Why'd you go on and gobble up Jeffers?" I picked up a stick like that was somehow going to protect my ass from a gator of that size. Lazarus could've snapped an arm like a Slim-Jim. That thought got me all choked up again, thinking about my best friend down in his belly. So I threw the stick at him, but he moved his head a little. The stick would've missed anyway, but Lazarus was just making me feel silly showing me he could move out of the way quick like that. "How'd you get your ass out here?"

I waited around on an answer and he just groaned, all mournful. Lazarus was supposed to be penned up at the Alligator Zoo-Park. He was the big attraction, the biggest gator for counties, maybe in the state. There was some rustling in the brush coming up behind me. Could've been a bear or some kind of big cat, but for sure it was just Tommy. I shushed him and pointed over to the clearing where Lazarus was camped. All I saw by the time I turned my head around was the tip of that big old tail scooting off into the woods fast as could be. Seconds. Two seconds, and he was gone. His trail of burps smelled like Jeffers and I swear I could see them in color. We chased him and lost him, then stayed out there all night, ate more mushrooms and drank more beer than a body could handle.

I cried like a baby and Pete roughed me up trying to get me to come-to. Andy disappeared for a while and we looked for him. Found him up a tree, straddling a branch and talking to a bobcat about what happened. I think. I think that's what went on. It all ended up kinda fuzzy, but we didn't find one piece of Jeffers or Lazarus. It gave me a little bit of hope in the worst way. I don't know when Tommy gave up and left. Once he saw Lazarus, he'd had enough to make up his mind about Jeffers' chances. Pete had to drag me and Andy out of there. I know that for a fact. I had every notion to stay and wait for Lazarus. I'd live out there if need be. Instead, Pete gave me a ride back to my house, where I ate a box of Hot Pockets and called Miriam. She didn't pick up. Instead, she knocked on my door.

"He gone?"

Her mouth was already purple with Carlo Rossi. She hadn't slept either. Maybe not in days.

I started bawling out my eyes and spitting a lot while I chewed my last Hot Pocket. I wasn't even hungry, but I snapped my teeth together and blew out the hot from the back of my throat. I tried to tell Miriam what happened, but just ended up honking and heaving a lot. I was a goddamn human puddle. It was all over. I told her there was nothing. That my friend was gone in the worst way. That I couldn't even say goodbye to some dead-and-gone, lifeless, cold body all swolled up with water, because I'd failed him in that too. I couldn't find him. Then I told her—I told her. I told Miriam what Jeffers told me.

"I'll be back on day three."

2

We left Jeffers' van, the NAILR, out at the springs. Miriam must've forgot that when she asked me to go find Aunt Becky and tell her what happened. She and Aunt Becky liked to pretend each other didn't exist.

Jeffers was gone. Judd dropped the rope and the big trick got messy. It took all the tools I had to get my piece of shit van to run, but I kicked it and jumped it and sucked gas out of the lawn mower and pumped it in that sonofabitch. I kicked the pedal and let it sputter, watched the redline get felt up by the needle and let it all loose in overdrive. I went to see Aunt Becky to give her the news about somebody I'm not sure she ever even gave a care about.

It started sprinkling, little drops getting bigger and flopping on my windshield like some lazy roadkill. I hit the switch for the wipers and watched the blades get thrown off, one after the other—somehow forgot Denny chewed them up, hanging on my hood in some fit of anger—the last one. Wish I could have flung her off as easy as I did those wipers.

I pulled out of the park and in to the morning light of progress. Swear to god there were folks lurking out there with chainsaws waiting to cut down every bit of my slow living. There was a river on the other side of the park and folks wanted a view. They wanted to look out on something they didn't understand. Wanted things to flow a little different. They wanted four lanes to get them there, too.

There were dogs racing and I knew where to find Aunt Becky, folding hand after hand and pouring free gin and tonics down her goozle at the track. I needed something to get me on her level, make me feel better. I found the perfect thing in a twelve pack and a bear balloon from the checkout line of the Winn-Dixie. The big bear balloon on the passenger side rubbed the thin fabric roof and stuck to it. He was good company. I knew it when I saw him in the check-out line, spinning with that big-old happy bear face on the one side and that big-old happy bear tail on the other.

"Cheers," I said, and cracked a beer. The bear smiled and spun and grabbed a hint of sun. My eyes found the road.

"I'm sorry about the air," I said. "It's been busted for a minute." The bear hugged the roof of the van and I missed a body in the seat next to me.

Half the time I didn't even need my hands on the wheel. My body moved better on the beer, as easy as that machine. I checked myself in the mirror, but a shadow hung over my face. I could move ten feet to the left to catch an inch of light. But my eyes were big and I wished they'd just be little dots.

I freed another beer from its friends, then a Camel from its pack, lit it and cracked my window. Camels lived in the desert. I'm sure I'd seen one. They looked like the woman in the median there in the heat. She had a gait like a mini-horse and was sucking down a two-liter of coke, fully tipped back. That stretch felt like the desert and the waves of heat made the red light sag like it wanted to drop right off its wire. I only stopped for fear of it falling.

"Can I get a ride?" the woman said.

"No room." I motioned to the bear.

The light changed, her eyes rolled and I pulled away. My van was all filled up, but everybody was thirsty. The bear drifted to the back, pressing against the glass. The wind slapped the headliner and the loose fabric rolled up in waves and the smoke streamed over them like a fog. It flapped harder, like it was clapping, and I knew it was for Jeffers. The dark gray puffer clouds cruising in got a little orange behind them and glowed on the fringe. Everything above ground got clear as day and quieter still. The moon still hadn't gone to bed. Goddam vampire. Being early was something I'd never figured out and the moon was just a sliver in the morning sky. I wanted to pick my teeth with it, but swished a last sip and watched it hide behind a cloud.

I had my van and I had that bear and my best friend was dead. I rolled my window up, grabbed the bear by the string and yanked him back up front. Maybe one beer too many for cruising, maybe one more.

I had another—the beers losing their company fast.

Another red light and I was waiting again. Jeffers was always telling me to wait. Telling me everything was right there in front of me. I pushed the palms of my hands into my eyes until all the world was blue. "Can't have you in on this one," he said. "Wait and see," he said.

The palm trees arched and wretched all their fronds out to one side. They gave up their dead pieces to the gutter. Wind blew in the rain and it came on for real.

I hit the pedal a little harder missed my turn, did a U, and ran a red light. I pulled into the dog track and my tires remembered how to stop. My hands were shaking.

I had to think of words for Aunt Becky. I'd wrap them around the string of that bear and let them go on and drift without me if I could. But she'd skin a man for less. "Talk with your mouth, Jimmy," she'd say. A man had to be there with his words. Not a few old letters strung together spilling out like the people did over there from the sliding glass doors when their pockets got emptied.

The drops hit heavy on the glass. Made it cleaner than it was. I never liked getting out in a storm. Figures Jeffers would make the whole world cry, and all on my back. I thought about every drop as they hit and wondered who could count them all.

A dark spot showed up on the headliner from a leak. My life leaked. The rain was too much for my wiper-less van. The metal just scratched up my windshield, leaving little channels for the water to sit in and laugh at me. I opened the door, letting my ownself get showered on. I yanked off my t-shirt and wrapped it around one of the wipers and let it go to work. When that seemed like it was doing something, I took my pants off and put them on the other one. That bear balloon must've had enough, 'cause he wandered out from the van, took him one look around my handiwork, spun a little and cruised out into the rain. There I was in my socks and undies chasing him through the parking lot, trying to get ahold of his string, but he was gone. I sat down right there in a big ass puddle and got to crying. Didn't even give two shits when a car rolled up and cracked its window.

"Just what in the hell are you on?" It was aunt Becky, gentle as always.

"Not on anything."

"Well then get your sorry ass out of my way." She blew some smoke out of the window. I could see she was drinking her wine out of a can. "Why're you naked?"

"I was finding you. I'm not naked." I looked down. "I'm wet."

She flicked ash out the window.

"Jeffers is dead. He gone."

Aunt Becky took another long suck on that smoke, wiped some wine off her chin while she blew out a cloud. She looked at me, could've sworn she was shaming my junk.

"Always leaving you, isn't he?"

She pulled around me, made sure to hit me with a wave of water when she did.

I splashed around in the puddle of oil and water and finally picked my ass up to walk back over to the van—pants and shirt mopping water back and forth across the windshield. Not doing a damn thing. I ripped them off and got to slapping them on the windshield till the wipers had learned something. Then I broke what was left of the metal rods so there was nothing but little nubs of motors spinning.

Jeffers was always looking for faith. He wasn't here. Faith in Judd got Jeffers gone. So I went looking for Judd.

The rain started letting up and the rooster got to crowing real hard. It was laughing like it couldn't catch its breath. Maybe it was the dogs I was hearing over the track walls. I had one beer left, and they simmered down while I drank it.

I got my wheels spinning fast to get dried off. They didn't even touch anything but the air around them. They burned up quick, then they were just choking on smoke.

Other folks would be looking for me, but I found Judd first—over at the outdoorsy store where I knew he'd be, staring through the window at the big stuffed animals with all their worthless teeth showing, looking like a kid with his nose pressed on the window. He was wanting things he wasn't willing to go after his ownself. Big animals that bit and chewed on folks. He didn't mind too much putting somebody else there, and him getting to watch. I saw him eat a couple times, his jaw moved like a moose.

"What are you wanting?" That was the first time I ever remembered Judd talking at me directly. More often than not, he'd just be staring at Jeffers or some mermaid, mumbling about something and ignoring me completely. "And why the hell are you naked?"

"I'm wet. Why'd you let that rope loose?"

"He told me to." I couldn't tell if we were looking in each other's eyes through the reflection. "Know you never had a say when you were helping him, either." He shuffled around a little. Checked his teeth in the glass. "I saw you laughing." He sniffed. He was always sniffing and looking like some scrawny old weasel. Before I knew what my hand was up to, it had that weasel by the throat.

"Jeffers was in his blowback," I said.

I got to sniffling then, choked up and started doubting things. Wiped my nose on my shirtsleeve and gritted my teeth as hard as my cavities would allow.

"Shit," Judd muttered, but he had his old rusty knife up at the bottom of my chin now and it possessed me to back my hand off his throat, while he spoke real slow. "Not. My. Fault."

"Sheriff will be coming for you." I took a step or two back.

"And don't I know it." Judd turned again to the glass.

We used to call it "blowback." When somebody would be giving the gators their treats, outside of the usual cups of cat food, really slinging fish down their gullets, letting them gobble-gobble on some mullet or some sort of bait fish that wasn't good for much else—certainly not for my eating—and all the sudden, that gator would let out that deep thud of a chomp and burp right there up in your face. The goozle would flare out like a lizard and their eyes got real big like you caught them doing something nasty. It was, too. They'd really let folks have it sometimes. Clear out a whole section of bleachers and make us wait on the next tour if it was bad enough. Folks weren't into sniffing that sort of thing unintention-ally. Jeffers could hold his breath a long time. He was real serious about getting good at it. Judd liked the smell maybe. They were the only two that would really be able to hang around after one of the gators did that sort of thing. I could never get into it. Chum. Buckets and buckets of chum. Breaths of blowback.

"You think they're doing a good job with the animals this season?" Judd said, blending in to the woodland critter display in the window.

I swear he'd lost it for sure.

"I guess I don't really give a shit."

Judd was tucked up all close to that window, nose nearly touch-ing it. He was looking wily, like maybe he was wanting to make love to a bobcat. I'd never put it past him.

"I like how they keep on bringing them back. We keep shooting them, hitting them with the cars, and they keep on stuffing them."

3

I came home to the park and a chop out on the river and I watched it for longer than a rested and sober me would've. I must have liked it for real because I was having a hard time figuring what I liked and what I didn't anymore. The winding dirt path through trees and homes made for just enough to get lost—unless a person had lived there his whole life. I could make my way through with a wet towel wrapped around my face. It was getting near noon and I needed to get back. My boys would be let out of school after a bit, so I got to sliming my way through the muddy roads.

The roads of the park were named after letters mostly, but one was a number. A to O, and the number 2, because that was the road the sewer pipe ran down and out to the river. Simple enough, but there were folks that still couldn't keep it straight because they never took the time to learn their letters. They would move in, looking real confused, and move out in the middle of the night a couple days or so later. Then I would go through their refrigerators.

There were plenty of landmarks. When enough stuff had been spilled on Pete's couch, we put it out on Sleepy Island, the corner of D and H, for the packs of dogs or folks to sit on when they got tired of walking or sexing. Whole lot of times I'd walk up on them snuggling up real tight looking satisfied and I'd think of Pete on

17

his couch trying to keep the fleas off it. Anybody had bedbugs or something funky going on with a mattress dropped it over there. You'd find somebody just about any hour of the day. Hell, I took many a nap on Sleepy Island, lots of good places to lay around and look up at the stars or some big-titty woman late at night riding me like a chopper bouncing over some speed bumps and every once-in-a-while, when the time was just right, standing up and "vrooming" like the morning won't never come. Sometimes, late enough, with that one little streetlight buzzing and the flies on it like a dimmer, I wouldn't even be able to see Denny's face. Long after she had shuffled on home, I'd still be laying there scratching everywhere and just breathing and looking up through the tall pines.

I passed the Gator Bank. It was another spot for that kind of resident. Over across K, near M, was where most of the gators liked to gather. They hung around huffing and grunting most of the time. I borrowed a couple of them here and there for tossing in peoples' windows, but most of the time they found their ways back home and piled up sunning. Gator Bank was next to the Moccasin Beach. Every time I heard somebody say Moccasin Beach, even myself, I couldn't help but think of them critters propped up on lawn chairs sucking back fruity drinks and rubbing each other up in suntan oil. They were slick, for real, and that was the beach most everybody went leaving alone. But there was some good fishing off that bank, so I wore my big boots if I wanted to catch something.

The woods were for anything else that needed dropping. Woods were over behind Miriam's place on one side. There was a mountain of car parts and swing-sets and rusted out grills. I tried to count the papasans one time and got disoriented. Plastic bags hung up high in the tree branches and swung better than the moss. There was an Autozone on the other side of the woods and sometimes the trees would get to glowing all eerie at night from the neon sign leaking through the woods. We used to get folks real high and scare the shit out of them talking about something coming through the woods. But there was something coming through. Progress was just a little slower and sneakier than anybody thought. It would find a park like ours sitting on some land butting up to the river. But we just did us and left right on alone.

My home was right around the corner. It wasn't anything much to look at. A van in the front yard to work on, two kids running around the yard beating each other senseless with an empty super-soaker, and two twin beds pushed together to sleep on at night. Between the barking and the braying, I slept alright.

The ceiling was low enough to touch and the roofs were flat. If I stood on the hood of my van, I probably could've seen clear over to the water if it wasn't for the tall pines. The trailers had their space in the yard. They had all their room outside.

I kept plastic on my windows and never had to worry much about the weather unless it blew in sideways. Then the trailer would get to rocking and the wheels up under would let me know they were flat. I'd pick up lattice skirting from the pines and the neighbors' yards after they'd got blown all out from under and around my trailer. The smell of wet wood sunk us all real deep in our place. We trapped the mold in the plastic siding and hoped for the best.

Every now and then I'd borrow a neighbor's leaf blower and blow out from under the house just to air it out. Cleanliness and godliness and so on and so forth and I was the devil. Animals and spiders and all sorts of shit would fly out from under at the sound and breath of that gas engine. Once saw a turtle hump up on a raccoon to get out of there quicker. I'd have to do it twice in a year with no hurricanes just to keep the banana spiders from repossessing my house. But it was easy living. The easiest.

I passed a stranger on my road, gave him a one-finger wave off the wheel and he nodded back, his face all lost in a beard and chin tucked down. I watched him in the side mirror, then hit the brakes. Everyone looked to me like Jeffers.

"Jeffers!" I yelled at him. He looked up, then over his shoulder, and for sure wasn't Jeffers. Not even a little bit. I tried to pretend for a second and come up with a question to save some face. We all liked our privacy, asking a question was asking too much.

There was usually somebody hiding out somewhere in the park. Nobody worried much about it. It was what we knew and felt comfort with. Sheriff Chuck didn't come through much unless somebody was grilling out. Sheriff came by that morning after Jeffers' big trick, though. I'd only been home a second when he walked in. He must've been following.

"Sheriff."

He was looking kinda crisp, except for the ketchup stain on his shirt from breakfast. I knew it was ketchup because I'd seen him at breakfast on the same day for nearly ten years over at the Waffle House. Same time as me and Jeffers, every week. He got that stain every time. Must've done something funny with that ketchup bottle to make it spit like that.

"Jimmy." The rooster outside got noisy and cockadoodle-doo'd.

Could've hung a flag off my pants from bouncing over the dirt roads of the park. I probably smelled like a still from drinking myself near blind. I noticed a joint on the counter and pushed it into the sink with a stack of papers while I held the door with the other hand. It would've been the least of my worries if it actually mattered. Sheriff knew I had a row of plants in the backyard. It was more of a respect thing.

"Whatchu know?" I knew the question was more serious than what he was sounding like. Carried the kind of weight that could make a man spend a year or two locked up. He kept his sunglasses on and little drops of sweat were racing down the lenses from the fat of his forehead. They hung over the rims and made a little waterfall. I wondered which drop would win and knew I was distracted. He started talking again. "Lotta shit went down last night."

He was telling *me.* I remembered running along the shore chasing logs that caught my eye, ratcheting the shit out of my lighter till it ran out just to get a look at a dirty old pile of clothes on the bank of the stream.

"I wish I knew, Sherriff. He kept me outta this one."

"I get it." He shuffled his pants like a sheriff would do. "The whole magician code bullshit. I watched the programs and seen the secrets." He shuffled in a step without me inviting him. "But this is for real, Jimmy."

"It ain't like that with this one. Jeffers kept me out. 'Sides, I can't make a gator not have eaten him." Sheriff just kinda breathed. I think he was sad. I know I was. "You want a coffee?" He softened a little like some butter left out.

"I'm good, Jimmy. Already had a pot at the Waffle House. Missed seeing y'all there." He was looking more than a little antsy.

"Can I use your pisser?"

"Course."

I started sweating as soon as he was over my stoop and in the door. There were enough drugs in my medicine cabinet to keep me high on the toilet for the rest of my days. That was my spot to keep them away from the boys when they were around. Sheriff came out a couple minutes later with a wet spot where the ketchup had been and a new bounce in his giddyap. I counted later, he only took a couple of my kids' Adderall. I kept the good stuff in laxative bottles.

"Been a real strange night, Jimmy. Even weirder morning." He kept adjusting himself, sweating again.

"Don't I know it."

"Nope. Weirder than you know." He went on and found him a cup in my cabinet. Poured his self some water. Downed it real quick. "Ladies at the Waffle House were tweaking a little."

"More than usual?"

He nodded. "More than usual. Seems they saw them a dead man. Maybe even served him up some breakfast." Sheriff sat down at my table. "You can go on and bring over that joint in the sink." I did. And lit it for him. He kept on talking. "Now a dead man, I can take that." He held his breath. "I get it. Jeffers went on and got himself ate by Lazarus and a bunch a bitties. That can happen. But them ladies at the Waffle House are swearing up one side and down the other that they served him up some hashbrowns smothered—no chunks. Said he ordered them different than usual. Put cream in his coffee, too."

That all seemed stranger to me than Jeffers being back from the dead. He'd said he'd be back. But cream in his coffee seemed real off.

"The ladies was saying they wouldn't of believed it, but for a row of teeth marks in his arm looking like a jack o' lantern had his teeth fall out." Sheriff leaned back and the chair creaked. That was the bad chair, and I held my breath every time he moved on it. Don't think he could've taken a spill out of that chair right then. "We ain't found a body."

I didn't think they would've. I thought that's what he'd come over to tell me. I would've been surprised. But Jeffers going around town showing up to his haunts being weird was something else. I was really wondering why he hadn't come by my place yet, if he was still kicking and all.

Sheriff got real serious for a second. "Jimmy, I gotta figure out what to do. People are wanting to know what happened. I can't go on and call him dead if he's going around showing up places, but shit can't go back to normal if he's gone-gone."

"Where'd those ladies say he was going?"

"No clue. Said I'd just missed him. 'Waffle House Rock' was still playing on the juke. Said he turned it on when he was headed out the door."

Sheriff had sat down to breakfast anyway. Man was always on duty.

4

Dear Lazarus,

*Tried to slide around the carpet like you, a big old alligator, but
my belly didn't turn yellow, or brown, or green. It turned a bright
raspberry milkshake and I drowned the flames in full-moon madness,
howling like a wolf instead of grunting and bellowing like your
brothers.*

Amen.

My dreams were wicked and had me wondering if I ate Jeffers
or if maybe he was going to be knocking at my door, making
that hollow tin sound because all the pulp-wood rotted out the
middle. But this was for real. I had a dull pain all in my lower stomach because one of my boys had just thrown a Flintstones bat at
my nuts to get me up. The aim might have been intentional, but
there was no way of knowing until I caught the boy that threw it.
I'd hit the bed around noon and it was still light out, so for sure
it was too early to be awake after going to bed for the first time in
two days. A couple-hours sleep made me feel worse than staying

up straight. But, folks had to eat, so I groaned my ownself out of bed and listened to my heavy footsteps squeaking on linoleum.

The floor bounced me along and I hoped the blocks up under the house were still holding. Sometimes they'd crack in half and it got a little easier to fall through, but living just wasn't that stable. That was a given.

I was doing normal life and feeling hollowed-out like my door. But it wasn't Jeffers knocking, it was my heart thumping heavy on the walls of my chest. I got to realizing that there were people out there looking for me. That was a fact. The boys were in the kitchen climbing on the cabinets, leaving them open after they prowled for food and found them empty. They could've been raccoons. Pets were easier than these kids, and I wondered where my momma was at to take them to the MacDonalds. I tossed the plastic bat at the boy hanging off a top cabinet, caught him in the ear and heard the squeal when he fell off the counter. The whole floor gave a double-jump and I got a little closer to the bathroom, walked into the yellow-wallpapered room and sucked in a breath.

Jeffers was gone. The thought of it tied my stomach in a knot and my tongue swolled up—all hungry and thirsty and antsy. I hadn't eaten anything but mushrooms in a while so I drank out of the faucet. I was just happy the water wasn't stinking. My hair was hanging all down the front of my face and trying to run down the drain, but the water was cool and had me feeling like the living again.

Some days I got water in my eyes and my vision would get real clear for a second. The world sparkled till I blinked. This wasn't that day. There was too much to digest and nothing in my belly.

"Jimmy!" It was Momma and she sounded funky. Like she got a

little hitch in her giddyap. "Just what the hell are you doing in there?"

I got off the toilet real quiet-like and looked in the mirror one eye at a time to make sure she wasn't standing behind me.

"Yeah, Momma? How you doing?"

"Hayyy!" She was talking way too loud. "This boy of yours has been out here crying for a minute. Says you hit him with a bat. Looks a little like he might of hit the floor. You do that?"

I heard the freezer door open. She was looking for Denny's vodka.

"Yeah, Momma. Deserved it." I called back to her, but her attention was shot.

I could've brushed my teeth, but it felt hopeless. There was a beer in the fridge that would freshen my mouth like a breeze from the Rockies and a Camel would warm it all back up to normal. So I pulled my bathrobe off the curtain rod and held my breath while I waited to see if the rod would fall. At least I was feeling like I looked decent with my face all wet. I walked out.

"Hey, Momma."

"*Hey*, Jimmy." She was grabbing the one boy off the floor by the arm. Sometimes I got their names straight, but Denny named them, and I still couldn't be sure which of her dead relatives they were supposed to resemble. The one had freckles and I thought he must've been "Teddy." I was thinking he might be the bat offender but the other sitting on the couch eating a Reese's looked a little less pathetic and a lot more guilty. I picked the bat up off the floor.

"You hit me with this?" I started asking. He was busy watching the TV and smacking while he ate the rim off the peanut butter center. "Hey! On the couch!" He turned around and I let loose, caught him in the Reese's and made a mess somewhere on the floor.

27

"That was the best part!" Sometimes they whined even better than Denny.

"Same thing I said when you woke me up."

Me and Jeffers were the same way as kids. Always annoying somebody, for sure.

Momma made herself at home on my recliner. Might have been hers at some point anyways. She found a bottle somewhere, and it looked cold, so it must have been stuck under some fish nuggets in the way-back of the freezer. I thought Denny'd taken it all with her, but Momma was sitting there nursing a fifth like a baby calf with her eyes closed. She didn't even cough when she put the bottle down from her mouth and into the crack of the chair.

"The chair's going to get wet."

"What happened with Jeffers?" She wasn't hearing me. I lit a smoke.

"Dreamed I gobbled him up."

"Don't be telling me your dreams before you eat something. Bad luck."

I held onto my smoke, let it eek out my nose. "Don't think I'll be eating him anytime soon. Looked all night. We couldn't find his body."

Momma winced a little, pulled the bottle back out of the couch cushion and gave it a sniff. Her body creaked—maybe it was the chair—when she stood up. "We're going over to the Macdonalds. You want anything?" The boys gathered on her hips like they were begging for some saint's mercy. I probably should've done the same with her offering a meal and all.

"Nah. I'm good." I just wanted to think. Fasting seemed like just the thing to help.

"Oh yeah. Found this taped to the door." She pulled a wet wad of paper out of her pocket and held it out. Clearly momma'd already read it. It was definitely from Miriam. Letters were scribbled in crayon with flowers drawn down the sides almost as good as my youngest boy could do.

Having folks over. Come on.

Momma wrangled the boys out the door and left it open. It might as well have been revolving, because just up the road I saw a van with a satellite dish humping through the brush. Momma and the boys drove off the other way and I kicked the door shut.

I tightened-up my bathrobe over my v-neck and made sure my Umbros were there, then scrambled for my shoes.

They were knocking before I could even dig my toes in. When I cracked the door, a camera tried to stick through the opening with the little red light glowing like some sort of goddam robot. I closed the thing back fast as I could. Attention wasn't my thing, for sure.

"Sir. Sir! I'm from the *Times-Union.*"

I got to fumbling and sweating a lot. I could hear some folks chattering on the other side of the door. "Just a few questions about Jeffers the Magnificent. About last night." She was using a real gentle voice, like she thought my bathrobe was a pet.

The knocking started again. It was a real thin door and it sounded like god out there pounding and I was thinking, *may be.* Then I felt like I was rude.

I opened it up for the woman but saw that camera light again.

"Gimme a second. I got to get decent." I said something like that and hustled down the hallway while they let themselves in.

I hid in the bathroom, looked through my cabinet behind the mirror, took a couple pills, and sat down on the toilet for a few to take some big breaths. Just what they were wanting I couldn't even wrestle. I was thinking about these two arms going back and forth holding on each other's hands real tight, going one way, then the other way, really just using all they got to try to pin the other arm. Big muscles. Like that movie *Over the Top* me and Jeffers used to watch on the tape player. Then I started getting a little further back there in my head, way back to thinking 'bout some thumb wrestling we used to get up to when there just wasn't another thing to do. Maybe it was raining outside and Aunt Becky kicked us out to the back porch so she could rock the trailer on its blocks.

"Sir, I know all about Jeffers."

I peeked through the hole in the door from the screw that used to hold up Denny's inspirational saying—something like, "You do you." I could see her big-ass ear pressed up against the door. Then she backed off a little. She was wearing full-on makeup, looking like Dollywood clown-school. Her pants were tight as could be and she kept dabbing her eyes for the camera like she was crying. Those folks were walking around my house filming. I watched her tip-toe around my trailer. She kept touching things and looking at her finger. Rubbed them together and kept moving her one side of her lip but wasn't saying a word. She bumped her leg on my couch and checked her pants for something.

It sounded kinda like it was raining in my head, but I was pretty sure it wasn't even possible. I ran in place for a couple minutes to get alive, punched at the wall a few times. Then I climbed through the tub and jumped out the goddam window. They must've heard me 'cause when I was running about neck-deep in the brush and halfway to Miriam's I looked over my shoulder. That camera was making sure it got every bit of me in my bathrobe romping through the woods. The news lady was yelling after me something about "good for nothing," really just a bunch of words stringing along after me.

5

I poked my head out of some cattails and looked around for a second, making sure that camera was nowhere around. Knew I'd have to spend some time checking myself for ticks. My legs were itching something fierce and I was covered in sandspurs. On top of all that, my white socks had turned green from a swamp puddle or something that I'd managed to trounce through and I lost my left house shoe. The back of my neck was covered with the filth of skipping showers and navigating woods. I needed a drink real bad and I knew where to find one. My bathrobe was looking like a fresh-washed puppy and I felt presentable enough to walk over to Miriam's.

I felt every rock of the dirt road and my steps left a mess of muddy prints. Every now and then I grabbed a palm frond and scrubbed out my tracks, jumped off the road and walked in the tall grass for a second just in case that camera was following me. Then I'd hustle my nuts and make sure I was holding together in my Umbros. It didn't take long before I was up on Miriam's porch.

Miriam's place was a turd in a tuxedo. She had new siding and a roof that leaked. No matter how she dressed it up with silk flowers and scented candles, it was still plunked down in the middle of the trailer hood. She did know how to make things look pretty, though.

There were all these cute womanly touches that Denny never could put a fat finger on. She had a gnome garden out front with a bundle of miniature houses showing all these smiling faces in pointy hats riding foxes, I would think, through the gnome woods. There was a collection of birdhouses too. But the squirrels ate all the birdseed, so I knew for a fact they were just for show.

I knocked on the door and sawdust puffed out of the frame. For sure, I thought about jumping down off that porch and walking around back, kinda wondered why I didn't do that in the first place. But then there she was. Bare-faced and streaks from tears splitting up her face like zippers, Carlo Rossi jug hanging by a finger. In all her sadness I forgot about that camera.

"I got your note," I said.

"You smell awful." Her voice warbled and she choked back a couple heaves. "What note?"

"This one." Somehow I'd kept it balled-up in my hand the whole time. I held up the ball.

"Jimmy, that's from a week ago." She snorted big snot.

"My bad. Momma just gave it to me." I dropped the ball of paper in the planter on her porch. "You still having people over?" She kinda shook her head. I couldn't tell if it was a "no" to my question or if she was crying again.

She motioned with the bottle toward the propped door.

"Come on in."

We walked straight to the fridge and she handed me a High Life then kept them coming on repeat for the next hour or so. I was thirsty. We sat just looking every now and then to see that the other was still sitting, too, till finally I talked.

"He disappeared." I was thinking while I was talking, so the words were kinda slobbery. "His ownself."

Miriam looked over at me, not looking like she was sure she was ready for me to have talked like that. "He did."

Miriam and me—we got good and drunk and more words came. We made us a plan about how we were going to remember Jeffers right. She knew he was supposed to come back and I knew it and nobody else had a damn clue, and there was just no way he would miss out on his own party. We guzzled our hope and we both knew somewhere down deep that it just wasn't going to happen. But we'd have that party anyway.

We thought all that for sure, but I don't know how we said a lick of it in the middle of drinking. Miriam and her Carlo Rossi. Me and anything that popped up in my way cold enough or fiery enough to make my eyes blur.

I tipped my bottle and choked back some grief, thought about Jeffers and communed with the next-to-dead. Miriam made phone calls and the door started opening, once or twice at first, then it just got propped as folks kept coming. There was still a little hope up in my head somewhere that he wasn't dead at all. I thought about his insides first, the scar on his collarbone from the handlebars of his bike, hidden from light by skin, healed over but forever marked up on the bone. That, in my mind, would never be exposed to no one, just the plush lining of a casket or a cavern full of fish and gators, hungry for a snack. And then there was his chin. I pushed him into the coffee table at Aunt Becky's. We were five. But he carried it with him the rest of his life. My beers told me I was logical, that honest thought said it's over, that there wouldn't be a casket.

Not necessary. For those of us that disappear in the caverns of a spring, thousands of years our elder and undying, there was no body to say goodbye to, only a wake. A three-day drunk. No need for an open casket with makeup done right, blush on the cheeks, hair combed in the most un-intimate way, a show for the affections of others. A parade to a plot and a mix in the soil to make a formaldehyde slurry. One way or another, Jeffers would have that. No family to bury him, but an Aunt Becky that never wanted him. Never asked for him. And a bunch of no-good friends trying to remember him by rolling joints on his girlfriend's kitchen table and blowing clouds of smoke in his pet gator's nose.

Lots of laughs to be had.

I thought back to Judd.

For sure, the sort of thing I'd do watching my best friend in the whole wide world dangling from a swinging rope and landing in a pool full of gators, was laugh. People saw me doing that. No doubt about it. But it was kind of like when the water fountain used to make that fart noise when a girl was drinking from it in middle school. No matter the threat from a teacher, I couldn't stop. Some things my brain just gave up thinking about. That was one of them.

Living was hard. It took a whole shit ton of work to keep at it. I'd wondered before if it wasn't easier to let off and be done with it. Just when Lazarus got him all of Jeffers in his mouth at once, I thought Jeffers had finally done it. He had all the answers right then. No more worrying about things like we were always having to do. But maybe it was just me worrying. Maybe I was always telling him about what was getting me. He didn't even seem worried flopping down from that rope and into Lazarus' mouth. Not even sure he really screamed, just that weird moan. So I laughed about one less worry I guess. What I felt was relief. When Jeffers went down in Lazarus' belly, so did my responsibility. He was the only person I really ever had to take care of or been accountable to. The only person keeping me around. I was always worried I'd end up with a gimp for a best friend, some invalid limping around, or me pushing him. Aunt Becky wouldn't a helped a bit. I'd be driving his van delivering chicken, hoping for A/C work and spoon-feeding him applesauce and mashed-tatoes.

So I drank to relief and I drank to leaving. I drank to Jeffers and to friendship and to every spine on the tail of Miriam's baby alligator Chubby and the number of ripples on the water when Jeffers went in, the number of bubbles that popped and the air they brought to the surface when they did. A beer for every one. The frogs spoke Jeffers' name and chanted it along with us as we toasted the minutes and the hours waiting on my semi-dead best friend. I wondered if the cool breeze was a ghost and what guilt I should feel for my lack of faith in promises. The carelessness of belief in magic was much at odds with the precision of an illusion.

6

Pete and Andy brought shrimp and dropped them in the pot, one at a time, heads-off batter-on and bubbling in oil. A sheen on the grease and I swear I could see visions of saints and deities, but maybe I was just hungry. We ate them straight from the pot, juggling shrimp and burning tongues and fingertips. The sun was golden for the time being, stuck and confused as to whether it should come up or go down. My legs were asleep and my head was more than a little woozy. I could feel the beer in my brain sloshing side-to-side like a wave pool and me on a raft, hoping some big-titty lifeguard might save me. The yellow light passed through slits in the neighbor's eight-foot fence. There were "No Trespassing" and "Tow Away Zone" signs tacked to it with rusted nails, pushed out from rot. The signs were sandwiched between Miriam's chain-link fence, which was about half the height of the tall dark wood with gaps between the poles here and there.

I knew what was on the other side of that fence. We'd jumped in the above-ground pool a couple times, only to get chased back over the fence by the neighbor's Rottweiler, Steve.

I finished another smoke and smooched the butt on a post. The new black mark joined a bundle of others. I held my cloud in for a minute, about as long as I could, then blew it out in the direction of the fire hole. Me and Jeffers were the first to call it the fire hole. We got to calling it the fire-hole 'cause that's really all it was to begin with. We had a single log and nowhere to put it, so we dug a little hole and stuck it in there. Lit it up and it grew to be a pit, but it never got called a pit. It was easy to imagine starting it up again in a few hours.

I had some doubt on whether or not Jeffers'd be there in time to help me light it that night.

Back in the house, somebody knocked a tooth out on a beer bottle. There was a little blood on the floor and Chubby was sliding through it like a slip 'n' slide. I found the tooth on the floor when I stepped on it. It was one of Miriam's friend's teeth and it was kinda decent looking as a tooth goes. Her friend's name was Tammy, and she walked up to me with a joint sticking through the fresh gap in her smile. She offered it to me, and I felt a little rude when I wiped the paper off before taking a couple tugs on it. The smoke settled the wave pool in my head and made my nose feel numb. When I closed my eyes, all I felt was heavy. I realized I was exhausted with some strange form of premature grief, maybe confusion. Maybe I was just really drunk and a little high. I found my way to Miriam's bedroom and flopped down on her waterbed. I hadn't showered in days and I caught a whiff of myself mid-flop. It made me slightly too aware of the stink I might leave on her bed covers, but she'd probably had worse in there.

After who knows how long, Miriam came in, put my head in her lap like a momma would and got her fingers caught in my hair a couple times trying to stroke my head before she stopped. Neither of us talked. We had the same thing on our mind, thoughts about Jeffers and the promise he made floating around like a little boat in the stream of our collective unconscious.

For sure, I dozed off a minute. I woke up and watched as Miriam pulled another jug of Carlo Rossi out from under her bed. She was in pretty good shape. She caught me looking and I played off me just being curious.

"Secret comes out." She smiled, busted. "My rainy day stash." Miriam sat on the edge of the bed and popped the top off. "I figure that's today." She tipped the bottle back and housed about a quarter, then handed it to me. I got me a swig or two and wiped purple on my arm.

A ruckus came from the den. "Dang it, Chubby!" Pete was yelling.

Miriam beat me to the door. I wasn't moving too quick, but we both slapped at the door handle a second trying to get that thing to spin. We spilled out into the hall, then the kitchen. The stereo was pumping out some Jimmy Buffet as hard as it could from one speaker. There were about six plugged in, but one doing the lifting, like some cripple that's only got one good arm but works it out real hard. Most of the folks had moved out to the back porch.

Miriam passed me on her way to the couch.

"What's he doing, Pete?"

"He's nippin'!" Pete whined and rubbed his ankle. The baby gator skittered along on his nails. Jeffers had given Chubby to Miriam for her last birthday. In my mind, that's like giving somebody a gun that grows up loading itself.

"Uh-huh." She still had the jug of Carlo Rossi in her hand. "Come 'ere Chubby, lemme get you something to nibble on." Miriam pulled a bag of dry food from the cupboard. It had a picture of some big-ass cat's head on the side. She put a scoop in the bowl at the end of the counter. I was sure Chubby would rather have the cat for a meal than the pellets.

She whistled at him, then called again. "Come 'ere, Chubby-chubbs."

The gator wasn't moving. Wasn't real interested in cat food when there were pickles around. Miriam left the food and seemed to feel better just knowing that it was in the bowl. Now all the blame was square on Chubby if he was nippin' ankles. He tapped along the floor from pickled hand to pickled hand, watching and waiting. Chubby got him a pickle here and there.

We never did do a daddy test on Chubby—or really any gator I can think of. But he damn sure looked a lot like Tubbs. He had those eyebrows that made it look like he was talking at me. Tubbs grew up after getting me fired. He was known for romancing and getting around the Alligator Zoo-Park. This one year, there was a whole bundle of the lady gators knocked up, and I swear it was all Tubbs. We'd hear these grunts all night round the park. Sometimes me and Jeffers would go over there late night once the bar closed down. It was dark, and kinda like watching a porno on my busted TV screen, but with the sound plenty turned up.

I got myself a pickle, the last pickle, from the bucket. Andy was stumbling around again. He was good at having a good time. His face was smushed up and his eyes were all squinty. He could do this seven nights a week, and he did.

"Oh shit," he said, laughing a little and holding onto a smile that looked painful. Andy pointed out back with the cigarette in his hand and missed his mouth when he tried to bring it up to his lips. He forgot about his miss real fast. The smoke wasn't lit anyway.

It started raining pretty hard and the folks on the porch moved in. Their boots and tennis shoes squeaked out muddy streaks on the yellow-ish linoleum. The windows fogged up like the briny pickle jar with all those new bodies moving in, and I pulled another beer from the fridge. We would need more before long. I looked out the back door and watched the fire hole get a good soaking. Somebody was smart enough to cover the logs on the rack, probably Pete. Puddles filled the holes between the grass patches and I thought about Jeffers dangling over the spring. I wondered what memory fluttered through, maybe just breezed by, when the thought of the end crossed his mind. Maybe he felt like he was so good he didn't even have those thoughts. But I knew him better. We'd been doing magic tricks, learning them and showing them to each other, since we'd first palmed a penny. He got better than me fast. Then he started doing what seemed like the impossible. There were things he did, like breathing life in a gator, I just couldn't come up with answers for.

Bundles of people filled every corner. Here and there another body would walk in to where I couldn't even see a wall no more. I found Miriam and Pete on the couch watching everybody mill around. Miriam had Chubby flipped over in her lap, rubbing his belly to chill him out. Chubby's tail was twitching across the tops of Pete's legs. I stood there a second before they noticed me. When they did, they just looked.

"What're y'all doing?"

"Talking," said Pete.

"Seem pretty quiet for talking."

Miriam just sat there, all purple in the mouth and hanging it open to keep breathing. She rubbed Chubby's belly nice and slow, I swear that ankle biter was snoring with his eyes open.

"Thanks for covering up the wood stack." I pointed out back, one finger off the can of diet Bud. "Guessing it was you."

Pete pulled his beer out from where he had it wedged in the cushion next to him. "No biggie." He scooted up a little and sighed. "Can you grab me one?" He shook the can back and forth to show just how empty it was.

I walked in the bathroom to take a leak and found a couple folks with their faces pressed on a pocket mirror. They looked up.

"Sorry." I said and closed the door back. I'd never seen real snow before. It seemed cold on the TV, and the thought got me dreaming about escaping.

I walked back out to crazy.

"Miriam!"

Some hoochie was yelling.

"This thing work?"

Oh lord, they'd found the karaoke machine.

The rain slacked off a little and I slid the door open for a walk out back. Life was getting crowded inside and folks were going back and forth over what song to sing. When they cut off the good tunes and finally did start singing some of Reba's Greatest, I got to watching the windows, debating how wet I could stand to be.

I found a smoke on the floor and snatched it up, giving thanks for my good fortune. I lit it up once I got outside and tried to take a relatively quiet moment. There was a white steel shed near the back of the yard. A couple of long cages were leaned up against the side of the back shed. Those things were never long enough to hold a big gator. Me and Jeffers had tried to cram all sorts of snapping lizards in those things and they never opened right, never did work the way we needed them to. They only ever worked for the babies as far as I could figure.

I could see through the window that Tammy was up on the coffee table singing some pop dance number. She was clapping her hands in between lines on the TV screen when the little ball was bouncing on the same word for a few seconds and she didn't know what else to do. Every time she sang a word, she beer-whistled through her new tooth-gap. When she swung her hips it reminded me of what bad sex could look like. The table made an awful racket when it cracked. She disappeared in the heap of railed-out whining and that song just kept on playing.

Back through the doors I sat hard in a kitchen chair. The legs spread a little and I listened to it creak. My face felt heavy and sagged under the weight of lost sleep. The scene in front of me was hard to watch and I might've closed my eyes. I wished Jeffers was there. He would've known just what to say. Maybe he even would've sung along.

When my brain turned back on, Chubby was on the table and folks were putting smokes in his snout. They were getting sad when he nipped at them, but then they'd try it all over again. Pete was looking at me funny and I remembered his beer, so I grabbed a couple more from the fridge. There were coolers lining the floor of the kitchen. People had been bringing tons of beer and plowing through it just as fast. I opened both and sucked the foam off the tops like nothing happened, then walked back over to the couch and gave one to Pete. Miriam was staring off, looking for some other planet.

"You really think he's coming?" Miriam turned to me.

I looked down for a watch I didn't have on my wrist. "I'm not holding him to a time."

I smiled a little, then drank about half my beer. Folks grazed around behind me. Munching on chips, getting drunk, dancing, falling back on what they do when they run out of direction and purpose. Chubby came tapping across the floor, a lit cigarette in each nostril and blowing smoke from his mouth like a goddam dragon. He made a lap around the coffee table, leaving a cloud behind him. I grabbed him by the tail, yanked the smokes out of his nose and got pissed.

"Knock that shit off, Andy."

"Godzirrra!" Andy roared. He was laughing real hard, hands up looking like claws and wobbling all over the place. Pete was getting steamed.

Pete went for Andy about the same time as Chubby. Pete and Andy were beating each other and Chubby was hanging onto Andy's shoe by the laces. Chubby knocked over a drink or three with his tail like they were small buildings and Andy's nose was leaking red all over the floor. Pete got his knees on Andy's arms and a hand over his brother's mouth. He let a string of spit dangle over Andy's face, then sucked it back in when Andy let out a muffled squeal. When he took his hand off Andy's mouth, he for sure looked like he was wearing face paint.

"Clown."

Pete was laughing and pretty soon Andy was too.

They had an understanding I'd never get. I never had a brother. Jeffers was the closest thing to it. Never had a fistfight with him.

Pete let Andy get up. Chubby had Andy's shoelaces stuck in his teeth and took off.

"Somebody grab Chubby!" Andy slipped around in his sock, chasing the gator-toddler around the house.

The front door squeaked and the spring popped loud enough to turn heads when it opened. Judd stood there looking like he'd spent some time in the woods.

"Miriam!" he hollered, looking crazed and maybe a little hungry.

"What are you wanting, Judd?" Pete said. Ready for a fight.

"Need to talk to Miriam."

"Man you are *fran-tic*," I said.

"Jimmy, don't get up in my business."

"Why don't you go on and take your bullshit elsewhere, Judd." Before I could say much else Andy had Judd's arms wrapped up behind him like they do on *COPS*.

"Come on, Jimmy. Get you some," Andy was calling. I didn't want the chance, didn't get the chance.

Pete had Chubby up in his arms, shoelace still hanging from his teeth, tongue rolling around bouncing off his yellow gums and looking ready for a taste.

"We're gonna let this here baby gator get you a taste of what Jeffers felt." Pete kept walking closer to Judd, close to letting Chubby nuzzle on him.

Judd started spazzing and caught Andy in his boys, hustling himself out the door. Pete tossed Chubby on the sofa and moved out after him. Everybody else did, too. Folks were throwing beers at him. Trying to catch him in the dusk, but their aim was off. Judd's arms were flailing and he kept yelling for Miriam while dancing around the yard. She walked out.

"What, Judd?" She barely looked at him. A full can caught him in the leg and he limped back to the tan dirt in the road out of the mud. He shouted hysteric like.

"I seen Jeffers!" He was hunched over, trying to pull up his pant leg and step back at the same time.

"You see him at the bottom of the spring?" she asked. "I doubt you could even get that far."

"No! I *seen* him. He was walking old Lazarus, right next to him."

"Whatchu on, man? I want some!" Andy yelled.

Pete threw a full beer, really good aim on it, and popped Judd in the ribs. The can spit beer back at us. Judd made a bad honking noise and heaved. Drooled some. Kept stumbling down the road. More folks threw even more cans after him. Some even tossed bottles. It got loud. Judd was hunched and yelling back. The bottles were breaking and crunching on the hard-packed road, spilling out and making for a messy drive if anybody ever decided to leave.

I swear I could make out what Judd was yelling off in the night. *He's back.*

7

thought I heard bleating, but it was just the speaker straining on a low note. That groan of a note seemed like it sucked the last of my energy for being inside, so I walked out back, watched the scene over my shoulder with a little bit of horror, like it might attack me on my way out. I could see Miriam wasn't too far behind. The steps were slick and I wobbled like a sailor on my way down into the backyard. I was sure it was just my tired head catching up with me, that I wasn't that bad off yet.

"That thing going to light?" Miriam held what was left of the handrail nice and tight as she stepped down.

"I guess we'll see." The ground was soaked. "Has to catch eventually, right?"

Having a fire was about self-preservation half the time. The bugs were no joke. When the first stars came poking through that shady sky, the no-seeums started getting me on the backs of my hands. The mosquitos pretty much gave up in that sort of weather, but the sand gnats got hungrier and nastier. The crickets and frogs were telling anybody who'd listen all about how wet it was in the grass and the woods could've smelled like Florida if I wouldn't have been trying to get the fire hole started up. Pete covered up the wood earlier, kept it out of the rain, and that helped out, but the ground was still slick and the stack of newspapers from the back porch was all soggy. Miriam tried to help by wringing them out.

"You pay for the paper, still?" I was striking matches one after another. I'd hold them on the wet log, set them under the log, on top of the log. Then I ran out. I looked over at Miriam. She had real strong forearms.

"I think they'll give it to anybody that'll take it. Haven't paid in years." She squeezed another one. "Sides. Jeffers liked to see what people were saying about him."

She was right about that. Jeffers didn't read about himself to get excited. He just wanted to know that folks were believing him. Made sure the papers got the story right. Miriam handed me another twisted up paper, all soggy and rolled over and good for nothing but spanking a dog or a kid. I stuck it up under the little teepee of logs I set up in the mud and took my lighter to it, held it there until it got too hot. Then I gave it a break and sat down. The railroad ties were wet, too. But it never mattered before and certainly didn't then.

"You want your beer?" Miriam knew the answer and was already bringing it over. She had her jug under her arm how she held it when her hands got tired.

"How're your hands?"

Miriam wasn't real conscious of her hands, but I could tell they were bothering her. She would wring them here and there like she did those papers.

"They're alright." She sat down, shimmied up for a second when she felt how wet things really was, then eased back down soon enough. Set the jug on the railroad tie and looked at her hands front and back. "They act up here and there."

The first real flame finally caught a log. It crawled up, threatening to go out all along, fading, then stretching out and claiming a little more wood till it was able to hold on. It grew fast then, taking on the whole log and starting to hit on the other ones I had set up in a teepee in the middle of the fire hole. I was just happy it happened. Miriam held her hands out to the warming logs and turned them this way and that real slow.

"Heat helps a lot." It was looking like the sky might catch fire before the logs did.

Sure enough, the cartoon heavens had about a billion and-a-half of those pink-orange fingertip wispy things shooting out like some big-ass jelly fish looking to gobble us all up if only its mouth was big enough. Death had come to see us and the sky was perfect ever since. The sun breathing its last, falling on the crispy edge of the tarpaper black creeping over us like a blanket getting pulled tight. But the stars were all just about out and blinking.

I dragged a couple of wet recliners off the side of the house that were more than a little sandy and slapped them good with a piece wood from the neighbors' fence to scare any critters from the cracks. The chairs were overstuffed to the point of spitting foam, like they were still seasick from the last big storm to blow through.

We lay back and looked at the stars. A couple of the park chickens started clucking on the fence and I knew the rooster would get started any second. They always got real turned around when we lit up the fire hole. I'd think after a billion or so years those birds would somehow get a little smarter, but it just wasn't true.

Somehow that fire licking the sky and bouncing light off the creeping dark made them think the sun was coming. I guess they'd be right eventually, just a little early. A few hours and it'd be coming back around again, giving us thoughts about how things were going to get better instead of worries about getting through the night. So I conceded and didn't throw a brick or a log at the rooster when the old cock got up there strutting and scratching like the cat used to when it was about to hit the litter box hard.

Pete came out of a shadow in the floodlight. He brought a couple more beers in his one hand, and a plastic "SEC National Champs" cup sloshing Carlo Rossi in the other. Set the beers down and straddled a log.

"You sharing?" I asked.

"You need another? Can't stand up how it is." He drank out of one beer, then the other. He was right, too. Don't think I could've been standing too easy then. My blood and alcohol would've run right outta my body in two single file lines, real steady if I would've been so much as cut.

Tommy showed not a minute later and sat on the other log. It was real quiet out. Nobody was talking much. Judd's hysterics reminded everybody why they were here. I don't think anybody was too big on that. It was hot inside, too. People were getting tired. We'd all been around each other a lot. Felt like my brain was smoked.

"Sheriff Chuck said he's hearing things 'bout Jeffers," I slurred.

I'd probably been just about dying to say that, but the thought had been ping-ponging around in the back of my brains. What was left of them anyway. But they weren't hard enough, just the soft stuff, so the ball wasn't bouncing too fast. Probably had a dent in it. "Said they saw him in the diner." I was telling a ghost story. My face would glow in the fire if I could get the chair to sit up, but it wouldn't do much more than lay straight back, so it was kind of like I was just whispering up to the purple-black sky. I saw alligators in the constellations and heard echoes of my laughter coming from the crickets in the trees.

For sure the world would stop spinning for a second and that could be okay. It might get started all over again.

"You been drinking on that Judd-juice?" Pete wasn't smiling anymore. "Had to damn-near pull you out of the swamp. Had a better view than everybody else."

"I'll be believing that shit when I see it. Might need to see me some gator's teeth marked up on him," said Tommy. He was real logical. Couldn't really blame him. He'd heard enough lies in his time from his woman alone. "Last I saw was, now you see him, now you don't." Tommy put his arms up like some drunk-ass alligator jaws and clapped them shut with a smack. Miriam kinda grunted and looked away. "Lazarus was fast, but he was belly aching all the way."

"Come on, Tommy. Don't go being a dick." But Miriam was looking away from me. Wasn't up to me to blow a trick. Jeffers told me and Miriam. Just me and her. Miriam looked all disappointed, like I kicked her puppy. I'd managed to make an ass out of myself. Jeffers always knew I couldn't keep anything to myself.

That old sonofabitch rooster revved up again. I pulled what was left of the lever on the recliner and the springs got real pissed while it groaned me upright.

"He was for real. Worked wonders. Healed Lazarus."

The whole lot of them had an empty look on their faces. Their eyes were dark and their mouths hung open like broken nutcrackers. Everybody needed to breathe, me included. So I got up and felt the world spin a turn. Crunched up my last beer can with a twist and fired it off over at that rooster. Missed him by a mile-and-a-half and the can just rattled off the fence. I was satisfied I even hit that much. A log popped and squeaked out a sizzle. The wet logs made blue flames here and there, purple smoke, too. I'd had plenty of smoke over the last couple days and I held my breath. Me and Jeffers used to hold our breath when we'd drive by a graveyard. I'd wonder who all I knew in there, and I'd watch his face wondering if his parents might be in there, too. That was what I knew he was thinking. He always held his breath longer than me. I smoked too much. He did too, but he practiced. I never practiced our magic like him. But I never wanted it like him, either. I let my breath go and started coughing, realizing that I'd been holding a joint all along, and so drunk I didn't know it was burning my fingertips. I set it down on the arm of the chair and it sizzled 'cause the chair was still wet. I didn't even know who passed it to me.

"I'll take it." Miriam held out her arm. It was white as could be and her green veins looked like a neon sign in the firelight. She was barely even there and I swear my chair was starting to float.

Miriam poked back in the chair and it creaked from the saltwater eating its bones as she leaned up. Her face was glowing in the flames, but they never looked like they could touch her. She pulled the roach up to her lips and gave it a pull, then drank from her bottle on top of the smoke. I thought the smoke was gone for good till it started coming out her nose. She didn't even cough.

Quiet as could be. All I could hear was the logs cracking and splitting from the water trying to get out. I looked in there and thought I'd see somebody sitting on the other side, hanging around the edge of the woods. Every time I blinked, I realized we were alone.

Pete was the first to talk.

"When'd you get to thinking he was legit?"

The fire grew and faded, breathed heat and memories. I saw gators and hats, hoops, tricks and miracles.

"Known Jeffers forever. You haven't seen what I seen."

PART 2

Alligator Zoo-Park Magic

8

The yellow Econoline had a big foam gold crown strapped to its roof. Thing was humping along down the road like a beached whale trying to find itself some lost water. Every time it bounced over a rut or a piece of road-meat, the crown shook, and I swear the van was laughing. It was the King of Creams. A bullhorn was taped to the cracked passenger side window, keyed, and blared Christmas songs from the tape deck. Kids came running from everywhere. Ones I'd never seen came trouncing out of the woods or out from under houses. Nobody showed their money till it was their turn, 'cause not everybody had the money for a pop. Showing your money up front was a good way to have to fight to keep it.

Me and Jeffers heard the King as soon as it got a neighborhood or two over. Noise traveled over the water, especially Christmas songs from a bullhorn. About the fourth time chingedy-chinging through "Dominick the Donkey," we knew that van was getting closer. When the van got too close, everybody started holding their ears, sticking fingers in and finding wax that couldn't possibly hold off all the sharp blasts of the holidays.

It was summer. The birds were gasping in the heat and the trees sounded like they were hissing. About a squirrel-an-hour would hit the ground, passed-out from heat and thudding like a piece of clay.

There was green peeking from the straw covering the ground, but most of it was poison ivy. The park was thirsty and the wildfires a couple towns to the west made every day feel overcast in the most suffocating way. My skin felt hot and swollen, like it might crack from the heat. The mosquitos couldn't even find a footing on my arm 'cause of all the sweat. We were cooking in a way that could only be settled down with an ice pop.

The man inside the King of Creams was wearing shades so blacked-out I was surprised he could see to drive. He didn't have a hair on his head, looked like it had made its way down to his shoulders and arms. The tank-top he was wearing was a window to the hair, and a sign down the side of the van read *Nature's Fruit*.

It was only ten-thirty but it felt like it must've been about a million o'clock. The temptation and desperation we felt for cooling off had made me and Jeffers near-crazy. We'd been hiding out waiting for the King for a solid two hours, plotting how we were going to get Creamsicles without having a dollar in our pockets between the two of us. While the other kids crowded around the side of the van, me and Jeffers hustled over to the driver-side window. I crouched on the ground and Jeffers climbed my shoulders, reached in and grabbed the keys out of the ignition.

"Hey-boy! Get back!"

The King had a tooth in his mouth and made the most of blowing his words past it. I'd only ever heard him say "one" or "two" before that, asking for dollars. That van rumbled around. Between the squeaking and rocking it shook like it might roll over and the service window got shut real quick. Kids were squealing about their pops, but that van was locked down tight.

Me and Jeffers split into the woods as fast as our eight-year-old legs would take us. I looked over my shoulder once and saw that old grizzly bear tearing through the woods. The King was wearing jean shorts and work boots, taking out tree branches, and I swear he took down a tree or two. His sticky hands got straw and leaves matted to them and the whole load of him turned camouflage. I ran clear to the other side of the woods, never stopping till I was nearly in the river. Jeffers was supposed to meet me there but didn't show. I waited around, felt sick for a popsicle and my best friend, and laughed a little between wheezes. Worry wasn't a real familiar territory for me. I'd lost all I'd never had and Jeffers was my only care. We looked out for each other, and I knew for a fact that things weren't right. I might've cried if I had an ounce of water left in my body.

I circled back real careful, listening for rumbles and growls, expecting maybe to see that man raiding a honeypot. But when I got back to the van, the King had Jeffers up by his shirt and he was done for sure. Jeffers had the King's keys held high over his head, jingling like a wind chime right there in the woods. Between the other kids' back-and-forth screams of *Lettim go!* and *Popsicles*! Jeffers and the King were having words.

"Keys." That man had his hand held out, sticky and matted like a peanut butter pinecone.

"Pop," said Jeffers. His other hand held down. Seemed like he was telling more than asking.

"Whatchu know?" That grizzly held tight on Jeffers' shirt for a second, eyes darked out like night, Jeffers' reflection like a far-off planet none of us would ever know. Then the King started putting

Jeffers down real slow till his toes touched the ground.

"Nothing." Jeffers kept his hands where they were. Keys up high, his other hand held out like he was going to let a dog give it a sniff.

"What kind?" The veins in the King's neck let up a little and he breathed around that single tooth a little bit easier.

"Pineapple."

"You sure?"

I agreed with the man. Nobody wanted pineapple flavor.

"That's the one on the sign. The Nature's Fruit. Says it right there." Jeffers read better than some of us and was pointing at the side of the van. The van creaked and leaned when the King got back in. He opened up that side window and gave out the pops kids had cash for. Those kids scattered, and pretty soon it was me and Jeffers left. Jeffers got in the van and handed me that pineapple popsicle out the side window. I got to opening it, concentrating real hard, getting the wrapper stuck on one hand then the other.

"Jeffers, you getting the pineapple, too?"

That van started going right about when I was taking my first chomp, freezing my baby teeth and making my jaws hurt like a sonofabitch. It was playing "Up on the Rooftop" and Jeffers was waving out the side window. Probably stood there too long, confused and a little hurt 'cause I was always the one wanting to get out of the park. I shook my head a second, took a minute to finish my popsicle, then went running out to the entrance of the park, trying to see if I couldn't catch sight of the van or at least where it had gone.

I ran to Aunt Becky's house trying to think about what on the earth I'd have to say that would make sense. When I got to the front door I banged on it for a solid couple minutes to no answer.

Her car was out front, along with some fancy number that probably went kinda fast. My hand was sore and covered with dried paint from sticking to the door, so I went around the side of the trailer and started climbing up the side to knock on the bedroom window. That shade was open and she was in there riding some man like a show pony, both arms grabbing him by the hair and every once-in-a-while screeching like She-Ra. I got to knocking on the glass and found a way for Aunt Becky to hate me forever. She near knocked me off my stoop with a look and maybe with her boobs all hanging out there, confusing my fantasies and whacking out my future relationships. She started throwing things and I thought maybe that man under her had a heart attack 'cause he wasn't moving much. I ran to the front door hoping to talk and she came out the door with a towel wrapped around her body and a bullwhip in her hand. She cracked that thing at me and I ran like a sonofabitch. She caught me a couple times in the pants here and there. I was yelling.

"Jeffers!"

"He can't save you boy!"

"Jeffers, though!"

"I told you, Jimmy!" It was the first time I think she ever called me by my name. I felt respected, just a little.

"No, Aunt Becky!" I was pretty short on breath, been doing a lot of running that morning. "Jeffers!" She cracked that thing again. "He's gone!" I got to sniffling and panicking for a few reasons, then she stopped running. She probably got tired, too.

"What?" She started pulling her towel up, re-wrapping it around her. Still had that bull-whip all cocked back and ready to go.

"He's gone. King took him."

I followed Aunt Becky inside. Sheriff Chuck was tied to the bed with some socks and had his hat covering up his junk. He smiled up at me.

"Hey, Jimmy. How you?"

Aunt Becky picked a towel off the floor and threw it at his face.

"I gotta pee." She hung the bull-whip up on the wall and went in the bathroom. "Tell the Sheriff." She didn't bother closing the door.

"Untie me, will you, Jimmy?"

I undid the tube socks from around his wrists and got to telling him the story. When I was done he'd nearly gotten his pants on. It was a pretty short story, 'cause I left out the part about stealing the keys. Aunt Becky came back from the bathroom, make-up on and hair did up.

"He left you, huh?"

The papers didn't really have much to say on it. Kids went missing all the time from the park. Alligators snatched up a few—bears, step-dads, clowns, snatched up others. Hell, whole families left sometimes, middle of the night. What should've been news, was when Jeffers came walking back.

It was either a Monday, or maybe another weekday, when he came walking up the road looking straight-up normal, same clothes he left in. Had some Popsicle on his face but not much else notable. I'd been bored as hell, and up he walked to the front of my house. Momma was inside passed out on vodka and the smell of her own perfume. Everybody was around drinking 'cause it wasn't a weekend.

"Just where the hell you been?" I probably could've said something nice and friendly, but he'd left me and it'd been real boring without him around.

"Been doing Pop's work."

"You left me here." I might have shouted that part. Maybe not.

"I know." He talked steady. I was the one getting all crazy. So I tried to calm myself a bit. Thought through what he was saying.

"You selling Popsicles?" I'm pretty sure my mouth was hanging open a little, probably poking out my bottom jaw and squinting 'cause of the sun and all.

"Nah. Doing his work." Jeffers was hanging onto a coin, a quarter— maybe a half-dollar. He kept palming it, moving it back-and-forth between his hands. It would look like it was disappearing.

I couldn't get much more out of him than that. I caught him up on some TV shows. Said he hadn't seen any. We walked down the road toward Aunt Becky's. I wasn't real anxious to see her but felt he should probably get on home. Said he hadn't been there yet. The crickets got real loud to the point it got hard to hear each other so we stopped talking. I looked over at him here and there and he just kept looking forward. The breeze blew hot, but Jeffers wasn't blinking. He was off someplace else but seemed alright enough. When we got close to Aunt Becky's place, Jeffers stopped. I noticed after a step or two.

"What's up?"

"Nothing." He was still looking straight ahead, not blinking, like he was seeing straight through that house.

Aunt Becky opened up the front door and it slapped the side of the house. She kicked a cat off the steps, sent it scrambling out in the brush. She had a frozen pizza in her one hand, a smoke in the other. She saw me and Jeffers standing there, ignored me for sure—but looked at Jeffers.

"Go get cleaned up, it's dinner time."

Jeffers and me, as close as maybe we were, didn't talk much more about Pop.

Never was another woman like Aunt Becky. Denny swung a whip like she was making spaghetti with two broke arms.

9

Jeffers' momma, from what I hear, was known for getting around the dens of the trailer park. Supposedly, she was real sweet and kind and a whole lot of men took to her. She was the better looking of her and Aunt Becky. When we asked, which we did here and there, Aunt Becky always said she didn't know who Jeffers' daddy was. But she always tacked on that he was up in heaven. This was a trump card she'd drop when she was tired of talking about stuff that just wasn't important in her mind. Sometimes, she'd get good and hammered and spill almost as much in words as she would in Boone's Farm wine. It was late, and it was Christmas, and she was sad she wasn't going to keep warm in some man's bed that night. Instead, she told us the story of the night Jeffers was born.

"Your daddy was gone, either in heaven or on the highway." Aunt Becky talked to herself, not looking at Jeffers. She probably didn't even remember I was there. She pulled her feet up in the rocking chair, knees to her chest and wrapped her blanket around her huddle. There was a rule in her trailer that no cups came into the den, so she brought the whole dang bottle. I remember thinking that bottle was going to fall right outta her hand when she passed out. She always passed out eventually. Me and Jeffers were quiet as could be. I was afraid if either of us said a word she'd shut up and we'd never get the rest of the story.

"Your momma was big as a heifer. We had to drive her around in the back of a truck to keep balanced. Couldn't put her in a car, the goddam thing would tip over." She took a big drink from the bottle and rocked a little. "We—me and *my date*—were driving over some big old pot-holed roads, trying to bounce you out of that belly of hers. It was like you were the one holding on real tight in there, not wanting to get out. She slid all over the truck, not hanging on a lick. Started to get a little afraid we were going to kill her when she started talking about needing a bathroom." Aunt Becky sighed. "Only about one or two stars in the sky. That kind of night. Where it was clear and near all-black. Couldn't see too far ahead, even with a good headlight. We pulled the truck over at the farm back off the lane a little ways. When we got around to the back of the truck, she had a bulge in her pants. She was wearing some tight jeans. I swear I think it might've been your head."

I laughed a little thinking about Jeffers the denim baby and Jeffers elbowed me in the ribs. Aunt Becky didn't notice. She was lost somewhere, flopping around in her boozy-Jacuzzi of a head. I got lost thinking about her in a Jacuzzi.

"Don't know how we did it. I weighed about a quarter of your momma. Must've looked like an ant carrying a dinner roll. I grabbed a leg and—can't remember his name for the life-a me—grabbed her other half. Had to stop here and there for him to wail about his hernias—I remember that much. Well, we got your momma to the pig barn and cut those jeans clear off with some shears. Thought they were painted on at first. Some big old hog came rooting and sniffing. Must've thought she was about to have some piggies."

Jeffers looked like he was on the other side of a thumping, like that car was just rumbling along about to plant him on its hood. His eyes were big and his jaw was clenched real tight like he did when things weren't quite right.

"Boy, we thought you and your momma were toast. But she cranked you out in no time. Named you on the spot and seemed happy as could be. The farmer that owned the place came down when he saw the light on in his barn. He had a shotgun in one hand and bottle in the other. Gave your momma some—you a little bit too, so you'd do some sleeping—then we finished the rest."

Aunt Becky smiled. Her eyes looked a little watery and she slowed down a bit, like she'd finally remembered who her date was. She breathed out and made the room smell more like a horse track.

"We didn't know it, didn't hear it, but your momma swore she heard some angels singing. She was getting nuzzled up by a goat, maybe one of those pigs, talking about how special she thought you were and such. She was losing it quick. But I'm pretty sure she got to hold you a minute."

Jeffers was up and out the front door not looking back. I was following and watching Aunt Becky's face while I walked. She didn't move but for another drink.

Jeffers and me didn't own coats. We put our arms inside our short-sleeve shirts and walked down the lane to the quiet of the cold and the glow of the streetlight. On the ground, I spotted a cigarette butt with a little nub left and had some matches in my pocket. I stopped to light it up then shuffled a few steps to catch back up. He wasn't stopping.

"Get you some." I held out the butt, and Jeffers took me up on the offer. We got to the river a minute later and stood on the bank.

The moon was nearly full and looked big and heavy like it was sitting on the water trying to take a break.

"Happy Christmas, Jimmy."

"Happy Christmas."

Don't know if it was the smoke or our breath, but we made our own clouds around that moon. I'm sure it was the same moon every night, but that night it looked like it was sagging, weighed down with feeling so big and blue. I broke out a pack of cards and we played a few rounds of coon-can and froze our knuckles. Coon-can became too much work. I tried to start a small fire on the bank, but the straw was too wet for my match. Jeffers told me to pick a card. We didn't want to go home. He would have to sneak in the door to a passed-out Aunt Becky, stinking like loneliness and boozy strawberries. I wasn't sure that I had a home. I would be cold either way.

"Pick one." He was insistent and fanned out the deck. "It's a new one."

I immediately felt alone. Me and Jeffers had picked up magic together. It made us feel a little better than dirt. We had always shown each other how to do the new tricks before we did one. Jeffers never felt alone and smiled while he waited.

"Man, I'm cold." I was shaking a little. My hand was in my jeans pocket, but I was too curious to not, so I pulled it out to grab a card.

"Remember it." Jeffers shuffled the rest of the deck while I stared at my card, then the deck. I watched and he didn't take the cards out of my sight—didn't flip any over—just re-fanned them and held them out again.

I put my card, the three of clubs, in the middle. Jeffers shuffled again, right there on the frosty grass. He laid the whole deck out, smooth as could be, in one wave of his hand. Jeffers was always better than me at that. The smooth stuff.

"Think real hard, Jimmy." He made a big deal of closing his eyes and putting his head down. "Now, pick one."

I wasn't thinking about much but how cold I was. Didn't really think a card trick was the ticket in that moment—but I picked one. It was the seven of hearts. I held it up.

"Wasn't this one," I said.

Jeffers still had his eyes closed. He sniffed. I sniffed. Smoke. When he opened his eyes, I looked into them and saw a flame. We both looked down. One card from the line had a little black cloud coming out from under it. I swear the thing looked like it was wiggling. Jeffers picked it up by a corner then turned it around for me to see. He took a breath and blew on the three of clubs real light. It caught flame in his hand.

"This it?" He held it out to me. "Quick, light the seven." I'd never shown him the card in my hand. I caught the fire from his. "Throw them in the straw."

We had a good fire after a couple minutes. When we got warm enough, we took turns throwing cards to the fire, feeding it.

I know we both wondered if Aunt Becky's story was true, but we didn't mention it again that night, or ever. Far as I know, Jeffers never asked her about it again. Just dropped it like a bad drunk.

10

J effers worked at the Alligator Zoo-Park. I did too for a minute. He got hooked up when he was still in middle school. Somebody wanted him out of the house so they could spend a little sweet-time with Aunt Becky. Back then Aunt Becky was the hot fries. There's the regular fries, then there's the hot fries—the red spicy number that made you feel lucky when you scooped them from the Tiger Mart. Only thing I'd ever been caught stealing was a snack bag of the Hot Fries. They were trying to yank them away from me and I was grabbing handfuls. I knew I was caught, but I for sure was getting a bite. Aunt Becky was the hot fries. Now she's something like a crispy old curly fry. Kinda wormy in a way, but not soft.

Way back when, fifteen or so years, Mr. Cotter was busy getting divorced from a woman on the colder side. Mrs. Cotter was something like an undercooked Wendy's Fry dipped in a Frosty. A little thicker and not as sweet. Mr. Cotter owned the Alligator Zoo-Park. His woman felt he spent way too much time with the gators and was gonna turn into one. He was trying. I swear the man wore everything you could wear made from a gator. Had his hat and his belt, maybe his undies, I don't know, but it was a lot. Man had a passion.

Mr. Cotter was looking for some spice, so he went looking for Aunt Becky. Not sure where she was working at the time. It was always a bit of a mystery. Sometimes she came home to Jeffers' place stinking like booze and sometimes she smelled like a bear. Sometimes she smelled like a bear had rolled in some booze and cologne, then given her a wrastling in the sheets. Me and Jeffers were dicking around, probably taping bottle rockets to G.I. Joes and jamming "Rocket Man" way too loud on the record player. We left the back door open, wasn't any A/C anyhow. Aunt Becky didn't usually stick around the house too long. She was a busy woman and liked places that did have A/C. Whenever she stopped through, it was usually just to pee and I'd do my best to walk in on her. It was funny for a couple times, then she started getting pissed and would throw things at my head. That's where the scar on my left ear came from. But this one day she came in and started pouring herself a little wine from the jug on top of the fridge. Then she lit up a match and some smoke and had herself a little sit down on the couch. Jeffers and me, we fired off one more Joe—watched him soar to his grand finale—convinced he would find another planet or a tree branch high up, then walked in through the sliding door. Aunt Becky didn't look up till she hit that glass of purple for a big gulp.

"What the hell are y'all doing?" She polished off the glass waiting for an answer.

"Firing rocket men to the moon," Jeffers said. We were for sure trying.

"Hmph. They make it?" she asked, like she might consider trying. Aunt Becky half burped, half hiccupped. A cloud of smoke poofed out her mouth.

"No," Jeffers said. "They're more like them NASA rockets."

Aunt Becky motioned for the lighter in Jeffers hand. He passed it over. "Watch what you're saying." She pulled out another smoke and fired it.

"We salute when they go up," I chimed. I thought this was pretty smart sounding, real reverent to the Joes and the U-S of A.

"Alright, then." She held her hand up, totally uninterested, and shooed me away. "Go on home."

"Yessum." I started toward the door. "See you, Jeffers. Aunt Becky." Then the door started knocking. Nobody ever knocked around that house but me. That was 'cause Aunt Becky said I had to. Some sort of never-ending punishment. In fact, the doors were usually wide open. I looked back over at Aunt Becky, who shrugged, and I pulled on the handle. Thing never turned long as I'd used it. On the other side was Mr. Cotter in full on gator gear. Thigh-high chaps in green and brown blotches with toe nails and teeth on a necklace. He was the first man I'd ever known to wear earrings. I saw my reflection in the gold dangly balls. Later on, Jeffers told me they were some big old gator's balls got dipped in gold. He had pockmarks like manholes deep in his cheeks, and when he moved any piece of his face, the whole thing creased up like an accordion. I wasn't scared of many people. The ones I was afraid of had beat me down at some point. Even most of those I wasn't afraid of. But this man had me fearing.

"Hey," he said, looking past me. He chomped the butt of a cigar, didn't have a tip on it. He chewed it back and forth through his lips, making it wiggle and dance.

"Hey." I walked around him, head down, leaving him there on

the porch standing and waiting for his invitation in.

Jeffers told me later on that Mr. Cotter sent him over to the Alligator Zoo-Park after a couple minutes with instructions to tell them he had a job. It got Jeffers out of the house for a few hours at a time. Suddenly, he got busy. I had too much time and not enough G.I. Joes. My place was right around the corner. It was a dark hole of a trailer, with a room that I slept in here and there. One of my folks was around sometimes. Most times they weren't. Momma couldn't see or drive without her bottle, and I spent most of my time elsewhere.

I went to see Jeffers nearly every single day. He started out hosing the bird shit off the docks and landings. The seabirds ate what the gators didn't get around to, then delivered it back on the wooden walkways around the gator pens. I helped him scrub the white rings that were left when the milky piles were hosed away.

It seemed like Jeffers got promoted a couple times in the first month, nearly every single time Mr. Cotter visited with Aunt Becky. By the second month he was feeding the gators buckets full of cat food and shooting sea birds in the butt with a pellet gun. I usually got over to the Alligator Zoo-Park about the time that Jeffers was loading up the bucket. It was a solid twenty-five-minute bike ride over to the park. By the time I rolled up I was always near dying for a hose drink and some shade.

Eventually I got picked up for work, too. Any time Jeffers got moved up to another job, I took over the older, shittier job. Bleaching bathrooms, cleaning tanks, scooping ice cream—I did it all— sometimes in the same day. None of it was beyond me. I didn't know I was supposed to get paid at first, till they handed me a check.

Me and Jeffers took our pay and picked up a few Hustler magazines and a box of Ritz Crackers. We paid double to have Aunt Becky pick us up some beers. When we woke up the next morning there was a pile of crumbs and beer cans. We could've done push-ups with no hands.

It was a Saturday, real busy, when shit went south for me. We were at least five years into working at the Zoo-Park. I was still cleaning tanks. Jeffers was feeding the gators and helping out Judd, the big-time gator trainer. He was massaging the big gators hind legs before the shows and clipping their toenails. I'd just finished cleaning the baby flying squirrels litter box over in the "hot room" when I saw a tail slipping under the door. I knew a gator tail for sure when I saw one. This one was little, like a whip, and I knew sure-as-shit it didn't need to be there on the other side of the door. When I opened it quick, the little bastard came running at me, all three feet of him, stripes around his eyes looking like eyebrows, mouth wide open and hissing like a possum. I stumbled because those teeth—while small—can still give you a permanent tattoo.

I swear the little bastard stopped hissing for a second and laughed all the way out the door and into the park. I grabbed a net and took my time following it out the swinging door into the park. Didn't want that guy waiting for me on the other side. When I started hearing the squeals and screams of some kids, I knew he'd moved on. There was a steady trail of field-trippers standing on benches and chairs, some hanging on railings and looking all weird and wild-eyed. I hustled past the Mermaid Tank, then happened across the first casualty—a bundle of feathers and a streak of red leading into the parrot cage. He must've been just small enough to make it in. After that I found a flying squirrel limping along missing a leg, leaving a trail and looking like supper. A sea-bird snatched him up before I could get him to safety. A recorded announcement came over the loudspeaker. It kept playing on repeat:

"Good afternoon, Alligator Zoo-Park friends! Please find some high ground. One of our friendly critters is hustling around looking for a snack. Don't let your ankles be it. Thank you, and enjoy your day!"

It was just about the friendliest fright I think a person could ever hear.

Jeffers was over in the big den looking all official in his safari suit and Alligator Zoo-Park mesh hat. The main den was like a gladiator pit. The gators were surrounded by a five-foot wall, then a fence with some chicken wire. Inside, the gators just had a bunch of stuff to lay around on. There were little concrete islands for them to cook their bellies on and a lazy river to float around in when it was time to cool off. There were some stacks and piles of "green turds"—that's what we called the big old gators that didn't move much—and Jeffers was prodding them in the snouts, getting them to exercise. Really, he was just flopping them around. When they get that big, hot, and sassy, they just don't feel like they have to do that much anymore. They lay their heads on each other's tails to cool their jowls and move their eyes here and there. The only time the big turds move is when they smell a fish or some cat food. But even for the cat food they don't move much more than to open their mouth knowing it'll get thrown right down their throat.

So Jeffers was in the middle of a feeding demonstration to

nobody when I walked up. He was trying to call all the tourists over to the main gator den. Some were jumping up into the bleachers and watching their ankles so as not to lose any toes. A good few trusted him enough to walk over to the fence.

Jeffers held a bucket of cat food in one hand and yanked on some big old turd's tail with the other. "Don't y'all be fearing no gator," Jeffers called out. A small crowd was gathering around and there was still some nervousness vibrating in the peoples' bellies. The announcement would blare here and there. Every time the announcer's voice hit a B-flat, this one gator would bellow a little bit, his goozle would jiggle under his chin and another field-tripper would wet their drawers.

I was still scooting around, not finding any signs of the loose gator, thinking about that smile on his face and how he was going to tease me right out of a job.

"Y'all, these things are peaceful as puppy dogs!" Jeffers was stroking one's big tail, then he grabbed a gator by the snout and tucked it under his own chin. It kinda looked like they were kissing and some kids snickered. He let it go and then tossed a handful of cat food. It pelted down on their thick gator-skins, sounding like raindrops on a leather roof. They dropped their jaws to the ground and waited for more. Jeffers underhanded another scoop to the open mouths. They just kept them open, not even swallowing. "I heard from that announcement that there's a gator on the loose out there! That true?" He pointed to the kids in the bleachers.

YAYUSSSS! they cried.

He cupped his hand to his ear. "Whatchall say?"

YAYYYYUSSSSSS!

"What'd y'all say if I told you I snatched that gator up in my hat here?" He pointed to his hat.

There was some silence, some, "uh-uh" here and there.

"Well, I did. And y'all have got to know that gator's name is Tubbs. He's a wiggling fool and likes strawberry milk just like you." He got some giggles. "Y'all like strawberry milk?" He pointed.

Some *no's*, mainly *Yayuss.*

"Tubbs likes cat food, too. Y'all like cat food?"

Ewwwww. The field-trippers called.

"Well, let's get him on outta my hat. What you think?"

Yayusss.

"You think the cat food'll do it?"

Silence.

Jeffers took his hat off and put it on the ground. Kids were standing up, craning and straining to see. Jeffers scooped a handful of cat food from the bucket and started sprinkling it next to the hat. Not a single gator moved. I watched their eyes and not a one twitched, so I watched Jeffers' face and he was still smiling.

"I just don't think Tubbs likes cat food as much as he likes him some strawberry milk." He picked up the hat for a second and shook it, put it back down. "Who's got them some strawberry milk over there?" A dozen or so little hands flew up. "Can I get a share?" A couple kids scrambled over to the lunch tables and popped open lunch boxes with unicorns and racecars. They scrambled back. "Jimmy, you think you can toss me one a them?" I thanked a kid and took the milk carton, threw it the twenty yards over to Jeffers. It wasn't a bad throw, but it wasn't great. The carton flopped on a gator. He didn't move. Jeffers wasn't flustered. He picked it up and held it to the crowd. "Alright now. You think Tubbs'll come out for this here?" Silence. Jeffers went about his work. Shook his hat a little on the ground, opened the carton of milk, then stuck his hand in the hat. The kids were holding their breath. I was holding mine, too. Jeffers took his other hand off the milk and stuck it in the hat as well. I'll be damned if that hat didn't start shaking and shimmying right there on the ground.

Sure enough, Jeffers pulled all three feet of that gator right out of his hat. Held him up under his arm and tickled his chin. Tubbs, that sonofabitch, looked right over at me and raised his eyebrows, teasing. I flicked my third finger back at him. I think that's why I ended up losing the job. Jeffers picked up that strawberry milk and poured a little down Tubb's gullet. That gator started honking like they do when they get real happy. I got to walking away back to get a mop and clean up the parrot blood and see if I couldn't find the squirrel. The seabirds usually dropped them and they don't actually fly that good. Before I could get to the cleaning closet, Mr. Cotter pulled me aside and yanked my badge off. Told me he'd mail me my last check. I told him I didn't have me a mailbox and he said he'd just give the extra money to Jeffers—he was getting promoted to "Magician."

11

Me and Jeffers had been racing vans for years. I got my first van when I found out there was a kid on the way in Denny's belly. Funny how fucked I felt. I'd been driving my little Nissan truck that Jeffers was always giving me so much hell about. I went and met him over at the Zoo-Park to tell him about my situation. Denny—like the diner—it was her daddy's favorite for the "Moons Over My Hammy." I liked it, too, but I would never tell her that. She got knocked up pretty shortly after we'd been hanging out in the back of the truck late nights. I was trying to think of how I'd let Jeffers know.

I walked up to the front gate of the Zoo-Park, something I used to not do. Even after I'd been fired, I always used the employee entrance. I remember the sign out front at the Alligator Zoo-Park. It had a big old picture of Lazarus with his jaws wide open, slobbering and looking generally pretty hungry. At the top it said, "Drop-Ins Welcome!" I thought that my life was hanging right over that big gator's mouth. Nobody cared, for sure. My daddy was a wrinkled veggie, sitting around the trailer all day waiting to see if he could die before the cat did. Momma hitched up with some dude a couple grades behind me when daddy finally found a pussycat with a little more fight. I used to think it was weird when she would sneak that boy a kiss at the bus stop but not even grace me with one. She wasn't that sneaky. I understood Momma fine as I got a little older, realized for myself just how complicated loving is.

But somehow I was feeling the heat of that gator's breath on my ankles, and I was thinking it was coming from Jeffers. We'd been best buds for so long, but I didn't tell him I'd been scrumping Denny. I just knew a woman coming between us would be the end of us being best buds. The thing about Jeffers though, he was always a couple ideas ahead. I found him and Judd over by the big tank. They were watching the mermaids practice.

"Man, they need some bigger tails," Judd was saying.

"The tails are big enough. They need bigger costumes." Jeffers was right. The mermaids looked more like manatees. They were the sweetest girls I ever met, but good lord they shouldn't have been flopping around in that tank. At least the alligators left them alone. They would drop down to the bottom and take a pull off the air tube, then float around, spinning and water dancing as graceful as the resistance of water would allow. It was terrible, if I'm honest with myself.

"Hey, Jimmy. What you doing?" I'd been staring at the scene for a minute watching their timing and synchronizing with the dancing and taking note of their mistakes. I wanted to jump in there and give it a shot, maybe drown myself.

"Man, I got some news." I was still looking at the mermaids. I could tell they were looking at me.

"You ain't dead." Judd was mighty observant.

"True. Sure as I'm standing here."

"Let's get us a coke." Jeffers saved me from getting testy.

Judd looked at his wrist for a watch that wasn't there. "I'll be in the den, getting the gators fed." He was trying to tell Jeffers what to do. Where he should be.

"I'll be there shortly." Jeffers nodded to move him on his way.

Me and Jeffers walked over to the snack bar stand.

"Two cokes please, ma'am." The old woman gave us the little kid cups. The red ones with the waxy coating that I used to rub my teeth on in between sips.

"I got this," I offered.

"I know you don't have any money." He pushed my empty wallet back at me. "Besides, this is free."

"They giving you free drinks? Thanks then." I raised my cup with a nod and had a drink, sucking on the weird flat ice cubes. We walked over to a picnic table that was kinda shady, had a seat.

"What you got?" Jeffers asked me.

"Man, I've known you a long time."

"The longest," he said.

"We've been friends that long." I was looking at my feet, starting to sweat a bit. Feeling real shabby.

"Uh-huh."

"Man, I've been sexing Denny."

"Denny? You sure?"

"Well, yeah. I think so." I felt a little doubtful in a weird way. "That's what her license says." I hadn't seen her license, but we had been in her class for every grade of school growing up.

"Ha. Sorry."

"About me sexing her?"

"Nah, for asking if you was sure." He was looking down in his coke. "Odd thing to say. Just caught me off guard."

"Don't worry about it." I shook my ice, looking for a little Coke left in the bottom of the cup. "Jeffers, she got a baby in her." I chewed on edge of the wax cup.

"Oof." He was smiling a little like Tubbs. "You're going to need you a bigger car." His eyes got all wide like they did. "Let's get you a *van*." He said it all breathy, like the words were just going to float on forever.

Jeffers was always right. So when he got out of work that day we went down to the used lot Pete's step daddy, Early, was running.

"Going fast is close to going to heaven. You ain't never felt it in that truck," Early was saying. We were walking through tall grass, looking at brown machines with specks of paint barely hanging on. When the wind blew, clouds of rust puffed up and I had to cover my face with my sleeve.

"I tell you, I thought scrumping was like going to heaven. I felt that in that truck."

Early let out a creepy old man laugh, wheezed and made the tiniest gap in his teeth. He kinda whistled and his throat closed up and got him choking—something like a, "heh-heh," but a smidge more gruff and freaky.

"You gonna need something that'll hump it off the line. Show some folks that *daddy* ain't messing."

"How you know?"

"Word gets around here almost as fast as one of these here." Early pointed to the silver Windstar. It was missing three hubcaps and pointed in the nose, like it was headed to the moon. The wood-paneled sides were beat in like it had already been there and come back. "Ain't no hitch in this giddyap. Fire off the line and keeps it straight like a big silver pecker. I'd put a bow on it for you, but it don't sound like you like to wrap it up."

Jeffers and me took it out that night, flooring it off the change from red to green, blowing away Camaros and shitty six-cylinder Mustangs. I felt ashamed of these kids losing in their muscle to the great silver rocket. The more rows of seats and cup holders they packed in the vans, the more horsepower they had to cram in the hood. Finally one of the kids in a Mazda limped up on our right at the next light. We'd blown by, floating over bumps and screaming out the windows at the colored haze of the lights changing against the black night, but finally had to use the brakes. They squeaked us to a stop.

The Mazda had their windows down too.

"Y'all gotta get that thang to the track." I saw them look over their shoulder, then they turned right. The Silver Rocket didn't have a rearview, and I felt a little suspicious, so I looked over my shoulder and picked up the blue lights spinning around.

"Damn." I was bummed.

"It's nothing, Jimmy." Jeffers wasn't worried in the least, but he wasn't driving. I for sure didn't have insurance, not even sure I had a license.

I pulled the van over to the shoulder and waited. Jeffers slipped some crusty old map out of the side pocket, started studying it real hard. The cop slowed and looked over at us but passed on down the road. Jeffers looked up from the map.

"They don't want to mess with a rocket ship."

The next day, me and Jeffers took all the seats out—except the front ones. Denny was pissed, but we still had space to do business when I put down a blanket in the back, and if we closed the windows and the hatch we didn't have to get bit by too many mosquitos. The sexing didn't last, but the mosquitos did, so I hung some fly paper across the back of the van and rolled down the windows when I was driving so it would push them all to the back, give them something to hang on to. The first boy came a few months later, like babies tend to do. I put one of the bench seats back in 'cause Denny lost her license just about that same time. She bumped some lines, then bumped my van and I called the cops on her. We tried to make up afterward in the back of the van and the flypaper caught the biggest bloodsucker it ever could've imagined. Denny had to get near all her hair cut off. Looked like one of them women that doesn't like men too much. She didn't seem to like me that much, anymore. That was the last time we tried to make up, just took us another baby and a few years to end the fight.

It seemed like the extra seat really slowed the Rocket down. Maybe it was my driving. It was alright though, 'cause by that time Jeffers had picked up his own rocket-ship van, the "NAILR."

12

Back when my van was still running right, I worked nights at the Casa de Chiné. In the cooler months, nobody got their A/C fixed. Just wasn't no reason to at all. I knew I'd get busy come about March when folks started feeling a little toasty and smelling the mold in their walls. In the meantime, Denny had habits. I had bills and a baby or two.

I picked up a few bucks here and there on track nights. My Windstar, my silver rocket ship, may not have been the quickest, but my skills in easing her down the track made up for her lagging off the line. When the light clicked green I'd start leaning over a little in the other lane, looking at the drivers all funny and crazed-like. Rules was no touching, but most got a little shy on having me in their lane.

Señor Luis spent his evenings at the track watching the races and snatching up the best drivers he could for delivering his wings. I got me that night job when I smoked a Chevy Aveo. Shouldn't have even been out there on van night. But it was there and needed smoking. I don't even think I'd got done cheering yet when Señor Luis signed me on the spot for a "sponsorship." That meant the Windstar got a topper on the roof with "House of China" in big block letters and I got me a night job delivering chicken wings.

I swear we could cook up the wings and have them delivered before the caller was even off the phone. He wanted fast and he made sure he got it.

When Señor Luis bought out Mr. Cho, the House of China became the Casa de Chiné. They kept the sign out front and everything. Just changed the name in the phone book to A-1 Casa de Chiné to make things official. It was the best chicken wing joint around. Those little wings was like bitty bits of heaven. The sound of fresh cooked wings getting sloshed around in sauce or flipped in some seasoning got me going better than Denny ever could. I would've had about a-billion baby chicken wings if I wasn't careful.

Señor Luis was crafty—about as crafty a businessman as I've ever known. He put the only other Chinese joint in town out of business just by putting "A-1" in front of the name in the phone book and selling sides of egg rolls with his wings. We should've been delivery and take out only, but Señor Luis kept his restaurant open. All the locals knew not to eat there, but every now and then there'd be a little confusion. A customer would insist on eating inside the restaurant. They wanted a menu, they wanted some té, they wanted one of the little cookies that told you the future. We'd make them wait for a little while at the front. They'd eat some of the ten-cent gum out of the dish and look at the empty aquarium that used to have the fancy fish. I'd hear Señor Luis screaming at nobody, knowing he was the one that had to work in the restaurant if somebody wanted to actually sit down. There was only ever one or two tables set up with menus and such. That was just for when the health inspector came down and got adventurous. If somebody was ever unlucky enough to sit down to a dinner at A-1 Casa de Chiné, Señor Luis brought hell to the table. Water glasses were dirty and got spilled, top ramen was thrown on a plate instead of lo mein. I liked to think of him as one a them snarling dragons that was tucked up under the glass on the table cloth. But having a restaurant made it alright for him to have a bar in there. If it would've been just a delivery place he couldn't have been sitting in there drinking Bud off the tap all night and day. Señor Luis had his stool and his ashtray and not a soul touched either.

Often times, I'd just be hanging on a red wallpapered wall with the gold dragons and bamboo houses, smoking a cigarette and drinking a beer when an order came through. Señor Luis' team of tiny men would fry up the wings and toss them in a bag. Pass a joint in the walk-in cooler and get back to relaxing with another beer. That routine went on near 'round the clock. I'm not sure the place ever closed. I knew folks that got the craving sometimes at six o'clock in the morning and had wings in their hand by 6:15.

Señor Luis timed everybody. Soon as he got finished putting the phone down, the clock was ticking. The kitchen would hand me a bag and I'd hop in the van. Grab a beer out of the cooler behind my seat and get to cruising. I kept the topper on my van all the time and it kept the speeding tickets away. Cops always let us go 'cause they knew we were doing our job. They never wanted us to not bring them their next round of wings neither.

My only shifts were at night.

The night shift was beautiful. The streets cleared out and I could really crank some noise outta the tailpipe. My Windstar gurgled and choked out exhaust, hummed all throaty when I found her top gear, squeezing her pedal down and feeling every vibration of reciprocation. The white signs read forty-five when my headlights found them and I wrapped my speedometer around to zero and then some. Shadows from the streetlights ticked by fast enough to look solid and I did work. My van smelled like delicious chicken.

Sometimes Jeffers'd come with me on the calls. We'd bring a few wings for us on the road and drink as fast as I was driving. If Jeffers was with me, we were breaking delivery speed records. Might as well of been the UPS of chicken wings. I'd take as many orders as Señor Luis would give me and he'd pretend I didn't have help. That's how we met Tommy. We were both driving nights. He had him a hot one, too. A later model wood-paneled caravan that filled up with kids every other weekend. On weeknights it filled up with wings and fired down the streets near as fast as me. We had ourselves a friendly competition and raced to make our deliveries. We tried to get orders at the same time on purpose and then leave tire marks in the parking lot. Tommy never believed a word anybody said. I'd always have to somehow prove to him how fast or how high or how drunk or whatever. It was probably from being left by his woman.

He said she came home and found him sniffing on some sharpies. Word was he wasn't wearing nothing but a fresh-dressed set of antlers, up watching late night hunting shows, slinking around the house, hiding behind the furniture and the house plants. Said he'd been doing it for years. That's what she told the judge, anyhow. Tommy doubted it all. Said he couldn't really remember doing the slinking. All Tommy ever fessed up to was wanting to be close to nature and liking to get a little wild here and there. I don't think his woman ever told him a true thing in his life, even "I do," 'cause she for sure didn't. Think she told the judge a lot of things poor Tommy couldn't believe, either, but she got to keep the kids. So Tommy filled up his time slinging chicken.

I guessed we all came up due at some point. The Casa de Chiné job kept Denny around for a minute. I could finally afford all those King Size packs of Reese's my daytime A/C job couldn't and get her some chicken wings on-demand. I'd roll home late at night, headlight hitting a whole bunch of eyes in the woods when I made my turn down the dirt road, finally lighting up the little cross stuck in the ground at the street from where the cat measured the tread on my tires. A bucket with numbers taped to it hung on a post where the mail got dropped. I'd have to race the afternoon showers for the chance to read it when it came out. Then the "No Trespassing" sign would show white with the red letters in the light. I trespassed plenty of times and others did me, too. Tape held most of the windows on the front of my trailer together. I'd step out of the van and see the glow of the TV through the clear tape on the front window. The palm scrub made all sorts of racket in the breeze. It'd been dried out and primed for a forest fire. Coming inside, I'd find the baby sleeping and Denny sitting there on the couch smelling like bath salts with Reese's painted on her face. She always said the same thing to me when I walked through the door. "Shhh," and, "what'd you bring me?" It was her way of appreciating me for sure. She would watch hours of exercise videos, like a promise toward the future. I think she was convinced that eating wings and sweating a lot was going to melt off baby weight. I loved her anyhow, I think. She was a warm body to sleep by and always left the toilet seat up.

13

J effers got an early call at the Alligator Zoo-Park for him to
come out and snatch a big gator off the green of hole number
six over at Shady Pines golf course. I came along—because. We
loaded up the traps and the catch-poles, a fishing rod, too, for if
they jumped in the water.

"Van's looking clean."

"I washed it." Jeffers laughed for no reason at all. In fact, I thought
it was pretty funny too. It was about eight in the morning and we
were pretty wound on 2 AM's, Tylenol PM, and a couple caps of
mushrooms we split for breakfast. We carried a wind-up radio,
one from the hurricane kit that we got with a Sports Illustrated
subscription ten or so years back. We listened to sports talk radio
when we cruised around. It was either that or mariachi. Me and
Jeffers cruised to the mariachi when we were good and drunk.
When we were only kinda drunk or high it was sports talk. I wound
the radio and we put on the mariachi station.

Ohmpa ohmpa ohmpa ohm

The morning sun and a mist of dew made the road look slick and
shiny like some big black snake winding over the nothing-hills of
marshy Florida. Every time we went over one of the little bumps
of a hill I thought we might get enough air under us to lift off.

I stuck an arm out the window and flapped it, hopeful for a boost. When I looked over at the speedometer it said 35, maybe 36, and I knew it had to be wrong. We were flying, lifted by some heavenly hand taking us to the golf course. Helping us along so we could provide a service. All that and I didn't need to get paid. This wasn't the work of man.

Ohmmmmmmmmm

I brought my arm back in and wound the radio some more. Too many more ohms and we may have transcended. The music got steady again and we landed at The Shady Pines Country Club.

The SPCC was a one-story, red brick house with a white steel garage attached to hold onto a couple of golf carts that worked sometimes. They occasionally lit their smoker on the weekends and only let folks in polo shirts eat the meat. They were all a little tubby from what I could tell. I imagined they must've been like a whole gaggle of pigs sweating like cannibals while they chowed on the pork. A squat looking man in golf shoes greeted us at the gate. He was holding a coke can and leaning on a golf club. I didn't see how the man could swing a club without spinning like a top.

"You here for momma?" He snorted out a half laugh, his bottom lip bulging like it was pregnant.

"Yup." Jeffers' eyes were all squinty, but he was looking sober. I kept my chin down and snickered a little.

"You boys are in for a treat. Missus is out on hole seven. That's a par three." He spit in his coke can. "Y'all done this before?"

That fella made us drive all the way back on the golf cart path so we wouldn't mess up their brown grass and armadillo holes.

By then, the NAILR was a rocket. Me and Jeffers took off the tail pipe and tacked on a bucket exhaust. It sounded like a tank stuck in first gear. We got back to the green in a hurry, spooking back-swings and adding strokes all the way.

We stopped a hundred yards out on the tee box and there she was on the other side of the pond. That momma was snorting and wagging her head back and forth. Telling us, "Uh-uh, don't you come 'round here." I know she was. There was babies around there somewhere in some bushes. You could hear them sounding like a ray-gun. We grabbed the poles and pulled the traps out of the back. I could see plain as day that she was too big for any trap— she took up half the green—so I grabbed the Duck tape instead.

"What you wanna do?" Jeffers and me were standing on the ladies' tees. He handed me a smoke, and I thought for a second.

"She's pissed." I blew smoke. "She for-sure doesn't like us. These poles won't be enough." I had my doubts. That momma was at least a ten-footer.

"Big girl." Jeffers held the smoke in. "I can take her."

"You think?"

He was scouting a plan. "You take the cart path. Just don't get in between her and those babies." Jeffers started leaning over into the edge of the pond, wiping mud on his face. "Let's do it."

I started walking down the path, half watching him walk around the pond, half making sure I didn't get too far along and get between momma and the babies. She was moaning, sounding not right as could be. Jeffers and me got up near her, about twenty yards, at nearly the same time.

"Make some of them baby noises, Jimmy." He was kinda

whispering, but not really. I started making my ray-gun noise and she turned to me real quick, staring at me, eyes bulging and rocking like she was dry-humping the green.

"Jeffers! I'll be damned. I think she's choking!" I whispered but for sure was yelling

Before I could say another word, I seen Jeffers running across the green. He jumped on her back like he came off the top rope. When he landed she shot that golf ball out her mouth and I swear the thing whistled it was coming out so hot. They started rolling after that, went straight down the hill and into the pond.

"Jeffers!" I was yelling, but they were already under. Just that quick. No man riding a ten-foot gator stands a chance when she starts rolling. All I expected to see were body parts and maybe some color-change water would start bubbling up. I've seen it happen—like *Jaws*, but for real and just as scary. But sure as shit, Jeffers head popped out the water first, calm as could be. He was walking backwards. Funny thing about him walking backwards like that. His feet were on the top of the water like what the girls do on the TV in their outfits with the skates. Could've been twirling, I don't know. About that time, momma gator came roaring back outta the water, too. She was looking real hungry and pissed, like women do.

"Jeffers," I whispered, "you moon-walking on the water." I was shaky.

"Jimmy, what we got for her to eat?" Jeffers was real calm and still whispering, even though we'd already made a ruckus to be heard two counties over. I knew there wasn't a thing to eat in the van, so I checked my pockets.

"How about these?" I held up the baggy of mushrooms.

"Worth a shot." He was on the dry land now. Looking back, I'm not even sure that his clothes were wet. "Bring them over here." He was probably twenty yards away now. She could cover that in about a second.

"Hell no. That woman is *ang-ry.*"

"Come *on*, Jimmy."

I creeped around behind him, put the bag in his hand. "That's the last of 'em, Jeffers. It'll be a long day without 'em."

Jeffers reached in the baggy and started tossing her a few at a time. Momma snapped them outta the air every time. Not a one hit the ground. "Just a big hungry girl's what you are." Jeffers sweet talked momma all the way up to the middle of the green, then over a little closer to the cart path. She was following him, mouth closed now, breathing steady.

"Jimmy, go get the trap." He sat down, and she flopped down next to him. Looked like they were about to have a tea party. Jeffers romancing that big momma gator and her just hanging around calm. "Jimmy."

"Yeah. For sure." I was walking backwards, too. Jeffers started making some ray-gun noises of his own.

I got back a minute or so later and the whole slough of baby gators was sitting around in a circle like it was goddam story time.

"These guys are ready to go." Jeffers motioned to the babies, a foot-or-so long a piece. I started picking up babies and putting them in the trap, sometimes two at a time. They were like little puppy dogs, just watching Jeffers the whole time. I think they were trying to jump in the trap themselves. Momma just sat there and

Jeffers was telling her about something. She was just smiling like they do. After the babies were all in the trap, I went and got the van and backed it up to the green. He told momma something and she just hung out there on the green, stone cold frozen, while we loaded the trap in the NAILR, then put a couple boards down for her to climb in. Her eyes were big as planets, and I swear she'd found another one to visit for a little while.

We stopped off to give the clubhouse the "all clear," then we got to driving. A little bit later I finally found some words.

"What'd you tell her?" The whole crew was calm and hanging out in the back of the van.

"I told her how good life could be. She'd been thinking about it when we were in the pond. We're all in it together." Jeffers pulled over into the MacDonald's. We drove through. It was thirty-nine cent hamburger day. We paid forty-nine cents and got cheeseburgers for momma and the babies. Jeffers and me got some Filet O' Fish and stood outside the car while we ate them. I broke up a few burgers for the babies and gave momma a couple of whole ones while Jeffers drove us back to the Alligator Zoo-Park.

Judd met us at the back of the van when we pulled up through the gate. Me and Judd never quite got on, but he'd taught Jeffers everything he ever knew about gators. I'm pretty sure he also got me fired the day Tubbs got out. Didn't feel like I was up to snuff. He was right, but I still didn't have to like him. I was pretty sure he also was feeling that one of the mermaids was hot for me.

Judd's momma was my first grade teacher, Ms. Scarlotti. I remember we had to bring in show and tell. I didn't have much. What I did have around my place—a couple hand-me-down VHS tapes and some spray air freshener—I sure as shit didn't want to bring in to show off. I thought about it real hard 'cause I didn't want to come in empty handed. I did what I knew to do, and made a new friend on the way in. It was the only time I'd ever volunteered to go first, but I was so dang excited to show off my prize. Ms. Scarlotti already wasn't super-keen on me, but she let me go. I grabbed my backpack out of the closet and brought it over to the front of the room. When Ms. Scarlotti saw the bag moving she got real curious and came over to check it out. I unzipped my pack and that woman swung herself 'round so fast the possum didn't have nothing to grab onto but her rear. It stuck to her, really sank its teeth in, and rode her around. The janitor had to come in and remove it. By that time, she had bare skin showing and needed a rabies shot. It was a little sexy in an odd way. I'm not sure I ever passed another test.

"New residents?" Judd looked at Jeffers. He liked to pretend I wasn't there. He was wearing a necklace made of teeth. I felt like that probably didn't go over well with the gators. Must've been like bumping into your dentist if he was wearing your teeth as a trophy.

"Sure nuff." Jeffers was proud and pointed in the back window. Momma and the babies had ketchup all over their faces, looking like clowns with big thick rows of teeth and noses that didn't squeak. "Real friendly ones." He was holding his crotch. "I have *got* to take a piss. Y'all got them?"

I nodded and Judd looked like he would miss Jeffers. The shocks on the van squeaked a little when momma shifted inside.

"You want heads or tails?" I felt like I was being kind, giving

Judd the choice. He just shook off the question and we played rock, paper, scissors, instead. I won and looked in through the glass to see how momma was situated. She was looking right back at me, so I went around to the side door in hopes of grabbing her by the tail. Right about the time I popped the handle, Judd opened the back end of the NAILR.

"Sonofabitch!" I heard Judd shouting, then a big solid snap of momma's jaws. She went right after him. "Y'all didn't tape her shut!" Momma was chasing Judd fast as she could and the babies were yipping like they do. I was feeling a little sentimental, like watching Ms. Scarlotti and my friend the possum all over again, when Jeffers and Mr. Cotter came running from inside.

"What the hell is going on out here?" Mr. Cotter was a little slower moving, maybe not as smooth and easy as when he'd been romancing Aunt Becky. "Oh, well I'll be."

Momma gator was looking right at him. She had Judd, who'd left the safety of the blacktop to climb the fence, cornered. Now she had her eye on Mr. Cotter and she rolled her tongue around in that big open mouth. She was quick for a ten-footer and we all knew what those teeth could do. Jeffers held his hands up to all of us and we quieted down. He walked up to momma, put his hand on her nose, and she closed her mouth up tight. Then he walked side-by-side with her into the Zoo-Park. Judd and me watched them walk on in, but still didn't move for a minute. Judd's pants were looking a little wet, and he held his hands down in front of them. I couldn't blame him if he pissed them. Mr. Cotter looked right at Judd, "How long you been doing this?"

Judd held his head down. My mushrooms were wearing off,

and I realized I was staring, watching a bit of shame that I wasn't really supposed to see. Mr. Cotter walked off back inside and I pretended to get busy, fiddling with this and that. I was about to ask Judd for a hand with the baby gators, but he was gone. I dragged that cage in myself.

14

Miriam floated in my head sometimes. She was for sure the best mermaid they ever had at the Alligator Zoo-Park. I remember the first time me and Jeffers saw her swimming in the tank. Jeffers had me come over just to see her. She was fresh off leaving home a few counties over and didn't even know to take a breath from the air hose. She just held the same breath she grabbed before jumping in. She held onto that one till she started turning blue and had to finally come up. Miriam was a blend of sweet and stubborn like that.

She was the only mermaid in the park to have a tail that actually fit. All the others had to squeeze into the thing till they looked like a tube of Aquafresh about to pop. For sure, she never stood a chance at being a mermaid long-term. The others, the manatees, were born into it. Some even said that a couple of them were squeezed out in the tank, water-birthrights bestowed from when they went swimming out of the womb, passed the turtles and otters to the top of the tank looking for that first breath. The mothers and daughters got tattoos on their lower backs that branded them as mermaids somehow—it was a dolphin jumping through a rainbow. The nepotism was deeper than the tank, and those girls didn't like being showed up by some skinny thing that came from a slightly bigger town. One of them even tried to dig up Miriam's parents, till they found out they were actually dead. She told me and Jeffers one night that they loved each other too much.

Miriam's daddy had worked nights at the Hardee's over back near Wasahilla. He was a good, fine man. Made wood models of shrimp boats and sold them at discounts in a booth over at the flea market. Her momma liked to drink wine, and lots of it. When her daddy finally started running outta steam for taking care of her, she came to visit him at work. He'd been working, hiring a bunch of young fine-looking girls for the Hardee's. She didn't take too well to that and decided to order her a Frisco Melt in the drive through. When she heard his voice coming through the speaker, training some fine young thing in the proper ways to fulfill an order, she had it. Took a bucket with a couple four-foot water moccasins she brought just for him and launched that sonofabitch through the pick-up window. They got him and a couple others in the kitchen before they were wrangled. Miriam's momma told all about it in the note she left before driving her truck off a bridge.

Miriam had been taking care of herself for a long time before she found her way to town as a sixteen-year-old that could do legal work, instead of bumming rides by giving rides. She had a love for nature and a sweetness deep down that didn't show itself when the Carlo Rossi ran out. Sometimes we thought she was drowning in that tank, when really her mouth was just a little purple from the bottle she kept behind the big fake treasure chest that blew air bubbles. She said the bottle stayed colder when she kept it in the spring-fed tank like that. Jeffers said he'd never kissed a more bitter-sweet mouth. I believed him. I think hers was the only mouth he ever kissed. It didn't take much to sniff the sweet scent of Carlo Rossi around her.

Miriam was real good at huffing things too, and me and Jeffers had to snake her out from under Judd's nose to get her to come out to the Village Inn with us. We saw her swimming out of the tank after the last show for the day. Miriam was hunched over the side of the pool, tail still flopping in the water, holding the purple jug in one arm and trying to pull herself up with the other. The mermaids usually helped each other out, but the other two got out and had already headed to the locker room to get hosed off.

"Little help?" she said, looking over at me and Jeffers. I realized we'd just been staring at her, waiting to see if she busted out of her seashell top.

"Sure thing." Judd came walking over seemingly from nowhere, like she'd been talking to him. Maybe she had been. Maybe we interrupted some other fate he was slinking into. Either way, Judd climbed the steps up the side of the tank and started trying to help her out. He grabbed for her free arm and all she gave him was her jug. She climbed over the side, feet trying to poke through the worn-out green glittering of her tail. Jeffers stood at the bottom of the steps while Judd stayed at the top. Miriam climbed down, half stepping, half sliding.

"Lemme get your tail for you." Miriam smiled at Jeffers, showing off her thin lips and purple teeth. Her brown hair was matted to the back of her head like a wet cat and her eyes flashed more light than the sun could muster in the evening. I watched Judd drink from the bottle, pushed aside and still waiting at the top of the steps for a moment that had already passed. Jeffers held her arm and walked her all the way to the shower. Judd climbed down the steps and pushed the bottle at me. I was grateful, even though I know it wasn't meant for kindness. Jeffers invited her to dinner with both of us. Me and Jeffers polished off the bottle of Carlo. We sat on the bench outside the locker room while she hosed off. She wasn't super-happy when she came out to the empty bottle.

"Where'd my wine go?"

Jeffers and me looked at each other.

"Judd finished it up," Jeffers said.

Miriam picked up the empty bottle, held it high and tipped her head back. I swear she stuck her tongue in there. Not a lick of shame in that woman. She looked over at us when she was done exploring the bottle. "We gotta stop and get more. Y'all driving?"

I stood in the back of the van and kept cranking the radio. We tuned it to mariachi and stopped off at the Tiger Mart for another jug. We passed the bottle of Carlo and drank it down before we even got to the Village Inn. Hell, we drained it before we left the parking lot of the Tiger Mart.

The Village Inn smelled like delicious should. We got skillets and ate them like there wasn't another meal to be had. Jeffers started trying to make Miriam like him a whole lot and made a butter knife pass through his napkin.

"But there's no hole in the napkin?" Miriam's jaw hung open on her last word.

"No hole. But it snuck right on through, didn't it?" Jeffers' eyes were getting squinty. Carlo had caught up with him.

"Do it again."

"Can't do the same trick twice." He was still holding the napkin up turning it back and forth for her to examine.

"I have." She snorted at her own joke. I think it was lost on Jeffers. He was too pleased with his magic doings. "How'd you do it?"

"Can't tell you. It's magic." He was grinning and staring at her. She was doing the same but looking a little skeptical.

I drank a whole pot of coffee and felt my heart do backflips trying to figure out which way it should beat. I think it was happy for the two of them. They needed each other. Jeffers had never had a woman smile at him that wasn't trying to kill him with a belt or a soup spoon. Probably not since his momma in the pig barn.

When we finished scraping our skillets clean and asking for more free biscuits to stuff down our pants, Miriam tried to leave without paying. We found out afterwards that she had never eaten at a *real* diner before. Jeffers paid for the whole meal. He was always generous on payday. Miriam probably decided right then and there that he was the gentleman for her. She was used to paying for her own taxi home after hanging 'round with a man.

Miriam made it almost a whole year at the Alligator Zoo-Park. She made it ten months longer than she ever did anywhere else.

Till Jeffers started his magic show, the mermaids had been the long-running favorite for the crowds at the Alligator Zoo-Park. They put on shows three times a day. It was a workout for those girls' lungs. I still wonder how some of them stayed so big. It must've just been their bones. Maybe they couldn't sweat any since they were already in the water. They just soaked it up like a sponge.

Miriam and the girls were getting all set for their second show of the day, the lunchtime show, when all the local businessmen and truck drivers who had their yearly pass would come over and catch a site of them girls spinning and flipping and flopping their tails. I think some of these folks had to have some running fantasies. I saw some of the same folks there nearly every single day. They weren't even eating lunch. The cooks in the kitchen were downright bored. They sold more gator nuggets to the children on the field trips who were supposed to bring their own lunch than they did to the gawkers and oglers.

Mr. Cotter had decided to spice up the Mermaid show. When the lunch crowd got their stamp to come in at the gate they also got a whistle, some really high-pitched number that would make all the birds fly out of the trees and the deer scamper for miles around. These old codgers and hound dogs were blowing their whistles all over the place. It was just the excitement that Mr. Cotter'd been looking for.

The mermaids started their matching arm waves and kissy-faces and such. The crowd warmed. I saw some faces get flush when they tap-danced on their split-tails bouncing back-and-forth. Their seashell push-up bras were jiggling, some more than others. When the girls flopped on in the water the whistling really ramped up. The folks that could, stood up clapping and blowing spit through their whistles in a frenzy.

In they jumped, splashing water out the top of the tank. The announcer got cranking and the music started. The girls locked arms down at the bottom, slinging air bubbles with their hoses and wagging their tails. They mouthed the lyrics to the songs like some underwater *Coyote Ugly*.

The turtles in the tank loved the air bubbles and would swim around trying to chase and chomp on them. Especially this one big old turtle named Ed. He was always swimming to the front of the glass and people would complain about him blocking their view of the ladies. They'd tap on the glass and mouth for him to move. Oh, Ed. He didn't like the whistles.

He was a big guy and was moving faster than I'd ever seen a turtle move, real spastic and disoriented like. He ran into the glass a couple times, but those folks just blew the whistles harder and laughed real mean. When the girls got near the finale for the first number they all grabbed each other's tails and spun in a big circle, making lots of bubbles. Old Ed came over too, frenzied and eyes poking out weird, snorting bubbles and snapping like some funny teeth. But Ed didn't have any teeth. What he did have was some weight and a desire to be comforted. Everybody always went to Miriam for comfort, I guess the turtles did, too. When Miriam and the others finished their big turn, arms spread out wide in glory, Ed decided it was about time for a hug. Miriam was doing her waves to the crowd, swimming real slow along the bottom showing off her wiggle. Ed just landed like it was nothing, right there on her back on the bottom of the tank. She busted up a whole cloud of sand off the bottom and knocked herself out on a rock. Took Jeffers and two others diving in and pulling Ed off her 'cause he was so heavy and upset. Didn't want to let his mermaid go. When they got Miriam out, she was bluer than a skink's tail. Took them pounding on her to get her to come back. It was quite a moment.

Miriam went on disability. Her whole new life had been in the tank. Said she couldn't go in the tank for now. But I did see her talking to Ed from the other side of the glass from time to time. The other girls couldn't have been happier. No whistles for the shows no more, though. Turned out the whistles turn a turtle's brain to jelly.

15

Thursday nights were track nights. My momma always took the kids. I don't know where Denny was, probably off losing teeth and eating Reese's somewhere. I had missed track night the previous week 'cause the youngest boy had a cold and Momma passed out early.

Jeffers wasn't hearing any excuses that Thursday.

"Go-on, Jimmy. We've got a time we've gotta be there." Jeffers was walking around the Windstar getting all pissy because it had a flat. Truth was, he probably already knew the end of the night before it ever even got started.

"Man, you know I'm changing this thing fast as I can spin the nuts. This ain't no pit row. 'Sides. Where's the NAILR?" I knew good and well that Miriam had it. He chilled out real quick.

I got it changed and we drank a six-pack on the way.

When we got to there, our buddy Hecho had just finished his first go-round. He'd won by the stubby little nose of his Astrovan.

"Townies here tonight," he said.

"Sonsabitches." I looked a few rows over.

City-boys came down from Jacksonville. They drove the late model numbers with the fresh-washed look. They looked wet even when they were dry as AA. I saw a Honda Odyssey with the sand paint job and dark tint. The townie had a V-Tech in that hot rod and a Jesus fish stuck to the back. He wasn't ready to lose. When he climbed out he was wearing a jumper with some oil sponsor patches looking like Evel Knievel's great-grand baby. City-boy took off his fancy painted helmet and had him a real nice haircut and a double-chin. His buddy was about to start a heat in a Toyota Sienna. The brake lights were bright on that bad boy. When he let off and hit the gas, I saw the stick-figure family waving from the back windshield like a tramp stamp.

The nice-haired townie started our way with what looked to be a stick shoved up his ass. Maybe his jumpsuit was too short to lay off crawling up. He was pointing at Hecho, not realizing nobody could hear a word of what he was mouthing. He got closer and I saw Hecho balling up his fists. Hecho was a flyweight gold glove champ. He buzzed around like a mosquito and punched like an otter in heat. I wouldn't have messed with him. Not even playing.

"Don't think for a second I don't see that extra spoiler." The townie pointed all pissy. I was looking at Hecho's van and not seeing extra anything.

"Luggage racks." Hecho said.

Hecho had one spoiler that looked like a fiberglass whale tail chained on with some heavy links on the back rack. Every time he hit the glass that tail flopped. I bet that van could swim if he got to hitting the gas and brakes just right.

"Luggage racks don't count, townie." I looked over at his van. "'Sides, you got a spoiler on yours I'm thinking is over height."

"Who are you?" He looked me up and down, think he was checking me out.

"Man that's gonna spank your ass like a baby." These folks never knew the house rules. Just wanted to come down for some cash. Hecho grabbed my arm—let me know it was his fight. Haircut had already forgotten me, anyways.

"Doze Sears lookin' X-Cargo's gives you plenty advantage." Hecho had him figured out pretty quick. "Why you really over here? You want to double-up?" I think the townie was surprised he didn't have to fight harder for the rematch.

Haircut walked back over to his Odyssey and cranked it, revving the engine like it needed warming. Hecho checked the chains on the Astro Van, let them jingle, made sure the spoiler was tight enough. They lined up and that townie gave the meanest look he could muster. He was all pent up with the frustration that comes with having too many expectations for himself. I kept those low for my ownself.

Sometimes, I wondered how Hecho's van didn't trip over a stick it rode so low, but it was burnt orange and looked like a flame rolling along when he dropped it in gear. It grumbled when he really cranked it, like it was getting poked with a stick and woke up real angry, then it was cooking up the street. He'd taken the little baby arm muffler off the last summer. Put a vacuuming nozzle-looking thing on there. The stubby nose went from looking puppy-ish, to downright hungry after he put in the gold grille with all the teeth in it. Like it might take a nip outta you if you walked a little too close. I stayed away from the front anyway 'cause I was never sure Hecho knew how to use the brakes. He was real antsy on the line.

When the light turned green, Hecho punched the pedal on that sonofabitch. That townie hit his, too, and they spun tires till they caught. The townie got a quick lead, it was just how his Odyssey was geared. That was a cruising van, though, meant for keeping the kids safe on long trips, watching movies with talking fish. His van got to sounding real sad, just whining down the black top. Hecho's Astro sounded like it had been locked in a kennel and whipped a couple times a day waiting on its dinner. Hecho had family there that night. He did every night. It wouldn't-a surprised me none for him to take a little advantage here or there, especially since there was money involved. But Hecho wasn't letting off no-how. When he finally took his foot off the gas past the end of the line, that whale tail flopped off and flared up like a sparkler on the Fourth. A big-time rooster tail of sparks flew up and we all got treated to a show. It looked like that tail was splashing all mermaid-like.

Haircut was hurt. The Astro nibbled on his pride a little bit. He came back over with his skinnier buddy who didn't have such a nice haircut. They wouldn't let up. Said a few things I would expect out of some Jacksonville folks. Brought Hecho's momma and upbringing into it. Really, he was pissed because he saw his money fly away like a poot in a hurricane. I tried it before, couldn't smell a thing. I was pretty sure those two townies couldn't either when Hecho finished with them. The Sheriff came by a minute later. I think haircut's buddy called him up.

Sheriff Chuck walked up all smiles looking at those two townies fresh off getting tenderized. He smiled at me.

"Jimmy, how's your momma?"

"Doing good, Sheriff. Got the boys."

"Good, good." Sheriff looked over at Hecho and those townies. I swear he slapped his knee and whistled.

"Hecho. You do this?" Haircut's nose was flat and he had a fresh set of clown lips. The other's ear looked a little bigger on one side. They were a mess.

"Sure thing, Chuck."

"Call me Sheriff, currently. I'm doing my work." Hecho's momma brought the Sheriff's department tamales and horchata on Wednesdays for occasions such as this one. She had six boys.

Haircut shook his head, realizing pretty quick the whole of the mess he was in. The other was busy holding his ear to his head. But they were lucky. Hecho had him enough in the first go-round. They wouldn't be back. I wondered what the one would be telling the mother of those stick figures. Chuck gave them a threat of a restraining order to take home with them.

Hecho hopped in the back of the cop car to make the townies happy and keep Chuck's department from getting investigated.

Things had gotten loud. The track nights had grown. Word spread a long way. Stewart ran the races out at the track—really just an old airstrip. But the city was finding its way out there. I could hear some jackass from Daytona over in the corner arguing with Stewart about trying to enter his convo-van in a race.

We got height limits! I heard from across the track.

"Luck, boys." Chuck saluted boy scout-ish and drove off with the lights on. Hecho waved from the back. I found out later they went to get some beers and shoot some cans off a stump.

The townies were still standing there with me and Jeffers. Hair-cut was bitching through his clown lips and skinny was telling him he couldn't hear a word he was saying on account of his big ear. Jeffers walked their direction with a couple beers and they were cordial enough. He then did the damndest thing, taking his beer and pouring it over the skinny one's big ear. The look on that man's face was something like pain and funk and fight and a billion questions all rolled up in one big hot dog of an ear.

"The fuck?" Haircut clown lips tried to rattle off.

The beered townie held the ear again, looking all horrified at me and Jeffers like we were a couple freaks. Then he took his hand away and looked at it, then at his buddy.

"I can hear." Skinny was pointing to his ear.

The damn thing looked completely normal. Normal size, no blood, a little beer wet. Jeffers was looking satisfied with his work and started walking away.

"Go on and tell your buddies," he said over his shoulder.

"'Bout some freaks!" I heard one saying, walking off.

I wasn't really feeling racing myself by the time all them shenanigans was over with. But we got real hungry when we got in the Windstar. It was stinking real good for some chicken wings.

"What flavor is that?" Jeffers was sniffing the air.

I checked the last ticket in my side panel, where I kept all the receipts from delivery runs.

"That's gotta be Jerk'n hot." I shook my head and tossed the question off, looked at him real serious. "What the hell was that back there?"

"Don't know, just didn't want him all beat up and can't hearing no more."

I started driving and a loose can was rolling around the floor. Pulled the van over to catch it and realized it was unopened.

I drank some down right quick and held it over to Jeffers. He shook it off and I finished it. Got back to driving.

16

J effers. You think a man could love another man?" I was saying. We were walking up to the Softy-serve—Miriam's new gig besides her picking up disability—getting deep along the way.

"You mean like wearing each other's class rings and letter jackets and stuff?" I swear he started walking faster. We'd been out of high school for years.

"Nah! I mean. Hang On. Watch out, that car's coming a little faster." We were trying to cross the street. Had to park the NAILR on the other side, so Miriam's boss lady wouldn't see us. She knew Miriam didn't get anything done when Jeffers came around, even told Miriam she was going to put up a flier outside with a reward of a free small cone if somebody'd call her up when he came around. "Nah, Jeffers. I mean like caring for somebody. Wanting them to be alright, but really giving a shit if they aren't."

"I guess." We were both huffing a little after jogging across the street. It was faster than we were used to moving and the cars didn't seem to want to slow down.

"I might get a blister from that."

Jeffers was the nearest thing I ever had to a brother. I think I loved him like one. I believe he felt the same. Miriam and Jeffers' kind of love was different. She loved him like a Hallmark card.

He was smitten, too. Jeffers must've loved her about like he loved soft serve. They'd been getting a lot closer since the Village Inn night. She'd gotten her a decent place. Been talking about how she wanted him to move in. Miriam saw him through the window when we were walking up.

"Does it always make that noise?" She didn't seem surprised, or at least she wasn't caring about it none.

"Sometimes, I guess."

Jeffers had us over at the Softy-Serve for 'bout the third time that week. The machine that cranks out the turds of white ice-cream had just ripped one while Miriam held her hand under it, slipping a star-shaped tube of soft serve into a waiting customer's cone. Miriam hadn't said a word to the customer. She was busy talking to Jeffers, staring, dreaming about Jeffers while he was standing right there. I was pretty sure she hadn't taken her eyes off him. The customer cleared his throat, some middle-aged man with a goatee and white tennis shoes with dark socks. He wanted that ice-cream real bad, had this crazed look with his eyebrows all twitchy and licking his lips a little much for my liking. Miriam was having to remake his order since she let the first cone flop all over itself by hanging onto the handle of that machine a little too long.

"You still like working here?"

"I guess." She turned around and handed the customer the new cone. Didn't even ask him for money. Just turned right back on around to Jeffers.

"*My toppings?*" the man in the shoes said, real snappy. Miriam frowned a little over at him, grabbed the plastic bin of sprinkles and dropped it over in front of the man. She wasn't concerned.

"He's a regular." Miriam didn't look back. The man shook some sprinkles out and left the spoon on the counter in a mess of spilled soft-serve and sprinkles. Looked like somebody murdered a clown. Another customer came up and dumped about half the sprinkles in a cup and walked off. "You were saying?"

"I was just asking if you still like it here."

"Oh yeah. It's fine."

The place was busy for around there—a little ice-cream shop in a strip center with nothing else around. But it was hot out. A lady came walking back in from outside, where she'd been planted on a bench.

She tapped on the counter a couple of times and Miriam rolled her eyes. Breathed out heavy.

"Yessum?"

"*Excuse* me for interrupting." I wasn't thinking she was serious when she said that. "Why's this on my hand?" She was a flimsy woman. Kinda looked like soft-serve herself. She held out her hand at Miriam like she should be squatting down and kissing on it.

Miriam walked over with a little sashay, showing off her rear for Jeffers to watch.

"How can I help you?" She crossed her arms over her chest like she wasn't really wanting to help nothing.

The woman was jittery, all sorts of unnatural. "I'm asking why this is ending up on my hand." Me and Jeffers were watching from the end of the counter. Seabirds swarmed a piece of something out in the parking lot. Looked kinda like a tornado.

"'Cause it's melty." Miriam was real matter-of-fact bitchy. "You should've ate it faster."

"I should've been able to finish this off before it's melting." Lady was damn near vibrating with mean. Had veins on her temples making her skull look like it was glowing blue.

Miriam propped one hand on the counter so she could gesture with the other. She was always talking with a hand or a bottle or a smoke. "I agree. Listen. You just go on about hoovering and we won't have no problems."

"I want me another ice cream!" The lady slapped the counter and the cone wiggled loose from her other hand. That got her engine rolling and she started banging her fists on the counter like a toddler. "I had to wait near ten minutes for you to give me this one!"

Jeffers was right behind her now. Like he knew some of this crazy was coming. He caught that ice cream cone. What was left of it anyway. Jeffers put the palm of his hand on that woman's forehead and closed his eyes real tight for a second. I wouldn't never of trusted that woman enough to shut my eyes. She looked like she might pop right out of her skin. But she stood there dazed. Propped herself on the counter. Jeffers opened his eyes and I saw him wink over at Miriam.

He took that cone on outside and squatted down with the gaggle of seagulls. And those birds just kept on coming till we could barely see Jeffers anymore. They were pecking and flapping at each other. Really just making a scene and Jeffers staying hunched right in the middle talking to them. Then he got up and they moved—just hopped right on out of the way for him. We were watching it all inside and nobody saying a word. The machine didn't even squeak a toot.

Jeffers walked back through the door and the bell broke off the quiet.

Then the seabirds started getting really freaky. More were coming, just swooping down. Some flew up real high, and dive-bombed a cat eating on some trash. One of them got in this poor old woman's perm, started trying to make a nest. Maybe it was just caught, but she was stumbling all over the place and trying to grab at that bird. Every time she got after it, the thing would get to pecking after her fingers. It was something else to watch. They were playing a game or something, dropping their mess on anything that moved. I thought at first it must've been the sugar. For sure, it was the sugar. Those birds just weren't used to that kind of bump. I figure every last one of them got a drop or two, or at least a crumb of that woman's ice cream. But then the seabirds started getting downright mean and mischievous. They were really getting after folks. I saw them for sure peck a little dog trying to walk along. Went after the owner, too. Got him right up the pants. They were flying in and out of traffic and folks were swerving. A couple of birds got nailed or put out a windshield. A truck went on and sniffed up the rear of another truck and the drivers hopped out to a worse scene than the wreck itself. One of those seagulls hopped in the rear-ender's shirt and started dancing like a sonofa-bitch. That other man went on and drove off, wasn't even worried about his car.

"Don't reckon I've seen haunted ice cream before," Said the man with the sprinkles. "You feeling better?" he asked that woman. She still wasn't talking. Can't imagine I would've had much to say, neither.

The seabirds got back to collecting themselves in the parking lot. The whole gaggle of them. We watched them and their little beady black eyes looked back at us.

"You think they're going to come after us?" Sprinkles man was talking again. "They're looking a little *hun-gry*."

But they weren't looking at us. I swear they were just looking at Jeffers. I saw their mouths moving, chattering about something that just wasn't right.

"They're heading on." Jeffers looked back at them.

A few of the seabirds started flapping and circling. Pretty soon the whole mess swarmed back up together in their own little funnel cloud. A couple flew over by the windows, exposing their little bellies and pecking at the glass, then found them a spot back in the mix. Fast as they came, the gulls flew off some place I was hoping was far away from the Softy-Serve.

Miriam whistled through her teeth. There wasn't a slurping noise to be heard. She put another ice cream on the counter for the woman, but that woman left it there. Walked on out, looking up at the sky the whole way to her car. Sprinkles man and the other couple folks that were left, started tossing their ice creams and walking out the door. Nobody could digest a thing. Past the lot, traffic was stopped. People ventured out of their cars and took in the damage.

"Want to go with us to the springs?" Jeffers asked.

I watched Miriam's eyes light like that lamp in my momma's place that didn't have no shade. She walked out from behind the counter and dropped her apron there on the floor. I'm not even sure she locked the door behind her. But nobody much was wanting any ice cream after that. Shit was haunted and word spread quick as melting cream on a counter top. I'm not sure if Miriam got fired or the place just got closed down. Either way, she was around a little more after that.

Jeffers drove us out to the spring. I sat in the back, cranking the radio and letting Miriam have the front seat. The mariachi blasted and I didn't bother to listen to the two of them talk. Didn't need to. It was their conversation. I sat on the carpet with my back to Jeffers' chair and watched the sun come in the back window. The afternoon clouds crept in, threatening rain, but cruised away faster than they came. By the time we rolled up on the spring, there was nothing but blue sky for the water to reflect.

I dropped my shirt on the bank, took my keys and such out of my jean shorts, and piled them on top. I walked toward the spring and took it in. We'd kept it a secret since we were kids. I couldn't even recall how we'd come to find it.

Jeffers would swim in his jean shorts, too. Miriam didn't bother to have us stop by her place to change. She was in her undies. It didn't bother me none. She was Jeffers'. I was probably still trying to work things out with the hoochie mother of my children, Denny, then. Pointless was the word I liked to use. I used a lot of words for her.

A few branches hung around the spring, sagging with moss— hushed and quiet and only swaying a little when a breeze snuck in through the rest of the forest. The water they shaded was darker than the pale blue and green of the rest of the pool. The bottom of the spring might as well have been an inch from the surface. It was magnified and the seaweed-looking greens waved at us when we stepped in the water. The spring looked like it had never been touched. Made me feel bad messing with it when I got in. It all looked so peaceful, and it was peaceful until that cold water splashed up my legs and my nuts sucked up in my stomach.

The only way to get the rest of my body in was to flop, so I did. Miriam was on Jeffers' back and they were giggling and splashing around, just generally being in love.

The water was clear, making the bottom look like the top and such, so I took a big breath and dove down deep toward the caverns. Bubbles came up from the hidden well making all that water happen. My lungs couldn't hold all the air they needed to get me as deep as I wanted to go. I wanted to explore the caves and find some treasure or something, never entirely sure what I was looking for, some mystery. But my breath was gone and I turned back, looking up to the surface. The light broke the top of the water and Miriam and Jeffers were swimming up above in their shadows. Miriam was still a mermaid. Her hair fanned out and her legs kicked. She sure was pretty. Jeffers glowed in the light. Everything around him was darker.

They came up for air about the same time as I did. We were all still human, I think. They were smiling. Miriam's teeth were whiter than their normal purple and I cared about both of them.

"I wanna do a trick out here," Jeffers said while he was treading water.

"Whatchu wanna do?" Miriam asked him.

"This is our secret spot, though. You don't want to be bringing folks out here."

"Not here. For sure. But, put on a show outside of the park. You know?"

"You going to tell me what it is when you know?" I'd been feeling a little out of the know on the things he was planning lately. On his new tricks, he wasn't letting me in anymore.

He dove down and swam around and the conversation cooled.

Jeffers had started scheming more. We both knew he wanted to put on a bigger show. The bleachers at the Alligator Zoo-Park were full every time he performed. He had a name, Jeffers the Magnificent, and a crowd, but no space of his own. He was worried he didn't own his act.

"I'm getting out," I said to Miriam. She smiled, but she knew I was feeling a little hurt.

I walked back over the shallow limestone, careful not to cut my feet and wishing I'd kept my shoes on. I sat on the sunny bank to warm up. The cool water made my skin go numb and I curled up, holding my knees in my arms, the sun on my back. It was hot and felt good to soak it in. I warmed up and so did my mood.

After a minute, Miriam came over and sat down. Everything about her was see-through and I tried to keep my eyes out on the spring. Jeffers was walking along the shore under the shade trees looking at things, probably planning something magnificent that he wouldn't let me in on.

"I think he's real torn," Miriam said after a minute of looking out there at him.

"Maybe."

"He lets you in more than me." She was right.

"We've known each other longer." I took a breath to let some warm in my chest. "He trusts you, too."

"I know." She smiled. "I love him."

"I know." I felt myself smile. My face finally thawed-out.

Jeffers gave everybody that wanted any, at least a small piece of himself. I had to think that me and Miriam got a little more.

I hung out on the bank into the evening. Jeffers and Miriam were in the van, lights shining out on the dark, looking out at a million shiny eyes. They were making out like it was every animal's business, and their moaning kept time with the gator grunts out in the bushes. I just kept on slapping mosquitos.

17

We were up late. Me and Jeffers always stayed up too late. Jeffers had a ten-inch TV with a built-in VCR and about sixteen tapes of *World's Greatest Magic Tricks Revealed*. We wore them all out. Didn't have a favorite.

"What you think about me putting on a show?" Jeffers asked. He'd been talking more and more about this. We'd actually already had this very conversation three other times. But the volume didn't work on the TV and watching these tapes got old, unless you were Jeffers. My biggest gripe was the purple spot in the middle of the TV from where we'd hit it as kids when the tapes skipped or caught up. But I didn't have a better one.

"You going to wear a mask like that?" The magic man on the screen wore what looked like a Mexican wrestler's mask they had down at the mexi-market. He fanned his arms all over the place, twinkled his hands this way and that, and generally didn't pay no attention to his big-titty woman doing all the hard work. Lately, I was watching her more on the tapes than I was watching the tricks. "You already *got* a show at the Zoo-Park." I had to try real hard to get some whine in my voice.

"I'm wanting to do something big." When we were kids we'd always talked about doing something like that together, but by then

131

I got the feeling that I was just the big-titty assistant—with no titties.

"What are you gonna do?" The assistant bent over to demonstrate that the box she was going to crawl into was solid. She touched the saw and it was really sharp. She mouthed, *ouch*, and covered her lips while they were in, *oh*. It was hot.

"Where you gonna do it?" Me and Jeffers sat about a foot away from the screen.

"Don't know yet."

The splash of about a dozen gators murked up the water around Jeffers feet. They were chomping their jowls and muttering like they do when they're hungry.

He had a couple of the eight-footers dressed like clowns. Sonsabitches looked like they were wearing lipstick and smiling real big. He'd been trying different things with the magic show, but this was looking more like a circus.

Earlier in the show, he had one of the clown-gators try to detangle some rings that were all inter-connected. Me and Jeffers had been reading about some tricks and that one had seemed basic. We thought it would behoove us to start from the top. Well that gator, not sure if it was Timmy or Bart 'cause I couldn't see his markings through the white-face, got tangled his-ownself and was pattering around with the rings around his neck, getting real testy. Jeffers gave up on that trick and we would get the rings back later. The crowd thought it was funny. They were a field-trip bunch, and it didn't take much to keep them entertained. But Jeffers took pride in his show, and I could see some lines of frustration on his face. He took it up a level, and that's why the gators were splashing.

A couple minutes before, he told the crowd he was taking a five-minute intermission and they'd moaned and groaned. I met him over by the water fountain when he came out of the utility closet. He was holding a hula-hoop that dangled a bag of beef jerky from a string in the middle.

"What on earth?" He was still having a drink but moved his eyes over to the hoop in his outstretched arm. "Shit, Jeffers, that don't look like a great idea. For sure isn't magic."

"Ain't seen the trick yet, Jimmy." Jeffers stood up from the water fountain.

"Something new?"

"Hang on." Jeffers walked to the utility closet. When he came back, he handed me a tape player. "Do me a favor. Press play when I nod at you."

"Alright." I tried to read the name of the tape but couldn't.

I followed Jeffers back over to the main den. The bleachers were filling back up with kids, hands full of hot dogs and cokes and popcorn. A couple of them pointed at Bart with the rings around his neck and the clown hat, half-strangled. His face paint was wet from a swim in the lazy river and now I could see his markings. Poor guy looked like his face was melting off.

"Ladies and gentlemens – Jeffers – Master Magician!" Jeffers said, and held out the hula-hoop. He took scissors in his left hand and trimmed a corner off that beef jerky bag hanging on the string. I swear the smell of teriyaki was so strong it weaseled its way over to the bleachers. The gators were flopping around in the water, rolling and wiggling with the odor of something so much more delicious than their standard cat food winding through their snouts.

They were already chomping their jaws, losing control of their emotions. Jeffers tried to get them to line up on the big rock next to the water. He wanted them jumping through that hoop. It was slow-going. The gators wanted the jerky, and they weren't sad to try to go through Jeffers to get it. They were following him around, his arm stuck way out trying to keep them off the jerky till at least one of them went through the hoop.

The kids in the stands were kinda halfway paying attention, halfway sucking down those hot dogs and hacking on some popcorn. Timmy the gator bumped Jeffers, telling him he was ready for some of that jerky and the clown nose taped to the tip of his nuzzle went squeak. I swear I saw a kid snort a stream of co-cola out his nose and ears when the audience caught that.

Jeffers was pained again. He thought he'd practiced real hard on his act and it sure wasn't going to plan. He grabbed Bart by the nuzzle and yanked him up on that big rock.

"I command you to jump, clown!"

Well. Well, well, well.

Bart, he jumped. He didn't go for the jerky or through that hoop. He took off Jeffers' stretched out arm. Hoop, Jerky, and arm all came flopping to the ground, and Jeffers was left there standing and looking. Those gators are ruthless when they smell meat, and the whole gaggle of them went after some piece of it. The arm and the jerky were gone in seconds. So were the kids in the bleachers. Their high-pitched squeals and screams sounded like a jungle or a playground with soda in the water fountain. Teachers were covering their own eyes and kids were hustling hot dog out of their gullets. The gators were chowing down, grunting. I saw one of them just standing there taking big gator-huffs of teriyaki out of the empty jerky bag.

I was worried about Jeffers. He still hadn't moved or even made a noise. He was patient for the finale.

When he heard the first, *Somebody call 911!* He took his cue. Jeffers yelled, "Ladies and Gentlemens!" He waved his left hand over his empty shoulder socket, and out popped another arm. Jeffers nodded over to me and I fumbled to hit play on the tape deck.

TA DA!!! blasted out of that mini-speaker then a recorded track of applause played at full volume.

I clapped.

Jeffers had lost most of his other audience. Three kids and a teacher, weeping with her chest heaving real good, stayed in the stands. I think the kids were in shock because they sure-as-shit weren't blinking none.

Word spread pretty quick from those kids. A news crew came over that night from up in Jacksonville. They asked him again and again how he'd done it, and left with a pair of baby gators and a small mountain of chicken fingers. The next morning Jeffers was all over the newspapers. Jeffers was the only person I'd ever known to make the papers without killing somebody or themselves.

People still called his right arm his "new arm" a year later. They liked to touch it. Jeffers and me were magicians. We had a code to keep. I saw the pork chop wrappers and super glue in the utility closet. He knew the evidence would disappear, along with his meaty arm. For a while I was of a mind to call him out on it. But the tricks only got bigger. I stopped being able to explain them.

18

I can't find them *anywhere.*" Big as he was, Pete could bitch and whine like all get-out. He was all nasally and it made him sound taller than real life. We were over at Pete's house, turning over cushions and looking through cabinets and such. He lived across the street.

NAILR was on blocks waiting on new tires and my van was out of commission—like always. We were trying to get over to dealer-Barney's house before he left town for jail and were feeling some heat on account of not having a ride. Barney'd been out on bail and was offering up a special deal on some caps and some hash. It was one of those once-in-a-month type-of deals. Jeffers was calm as a housecat. He'd been reading a lot about Indians and rising above lately, really just next-leveling. Wouldn't have been surprised to start seeing him lifting off or levitating or something. *Ohhhhming* around like a peaceful Rascal.

"Let's go fishing."

"What the hell are you saying?" Pete was red. I scooted between them.

"You want to go fishing at a time like this?" That was me. "Things is getting downright critical. Just look at Pete." Jeffers turned his head all-slow. He looked at Pete. Didn't say anything. Pete turned over at me, looking like he was ready to slap somebody. I didn't want it to be me. It'd like to kill me.

"Alright." That was Pete. Man soothed and calmed down in an instant thinking about fishing. I would've thought somebody rubbed rum on his gums.

"What about the caps?" Now I was whining.

"Jeffers's right. We still got a little while till he's got to report." He looked at his watch. It was around two. Couple of hours at least.

"It's slack tide," I protested. "They'll be eaten up and cooked."

"Doesn't matter. Need some fish for our dinner, too."

Pete was already headed out back to get his pole while he was talking. Jeffers went to get ours from across the street. I was left and grabbed some beers from Pete's fridge and stuck them in an Omaha Steaks cooler. Must've been a gift, or Pete was doing mighty well with changing oil at the ten-minute joint. We caught up in the front yard and walked down to the river.

Jeffers was whistling some bullshit tune, wasn't for real or from anything. Just whistling. I was stewing about missing out on Barney's doings. Pete was all quiet. We got down to the bank. Me and Pete baited up with some fake stuff. Jeffers was rooting around in the dirt looking for a worm, I assumed. We started tossing, while Jeffers was still over on the bluff dicking around. Pete hooked up first and pulled out the ugliest fish I ever saw. Some sort of mud sucker. He didn't even touch it, just cut the line and let it swim around with a new lip ring to show off like one of them girls at the Jacksonville mall.

"Really shouldn't do that." Jeffers had found him something and was hooking it on his rigging.

"Do what?" Pete didn't bring more tackle. "You got another hook?" Jeffers had a small box of them. Passed one over to Pete.

"Shouldn't be letting no animal loose like that with a hook in his mouth." Jeffers was sounding righteous. "It's a living thing." He threw his line in the water.

"What about the worm you just drowned with a hook through his belly."

"Wasn't a worm." Jeffers was smug. Smiling to himself, but really at Pete and his pissiness. "What are you wanting to catch, Pete?"

"Now, I ain't got no chance at a fish. I want to catch my keys and get on over to Barney's and catch flight." He fumbled with the hook and tied it on his line blowing in the light afternoon breeze. "What're you gonna catch with no worm and no bait?"

"Your keys."

Didn't have time to digest Jeffers talking. I hooked up and started tugging on something big. It felt like I might get yanked right off the bank.

"Those ain't keys, unless they're dragging a tire along with them," said Pete.

"Hells yes. Let's get us some dinner." I felt a little ashamed for not wanting to go fishing, for giving so much push back. Then the fin broke the top of the water and we heard that asshole cackling as he stole the fish right off my line. He even left the hook on there, like nothing was ever even on the line. I swear the dolphin was made to make a man look stupid as could be.

"That's a smart creature right there." Jeffers had the nerve.

"Fuck a dolphin." That was Pete. Least he took my side.

"Why's he got to be up in our cove? Stealing our fish?" I started digging for a worm, probably looking like a kid messing in the dirt like that. Had a thought and turned around. "Get your own fish!" I yelled after him. I might've even shook a fist at him. He popped one of his eyes outta the water and teased, throwing some sass. They were always messing.

"It's hot out, he's probably looking for some shade." Jeffers didn't seem to understand that I wasn't looking for his logic.

He was right about the shade, though. The big oaks on the bank gave us a cool spot. That dolphin out there was probably getting him a sunburn at least. I've seen manatees tucked up under docks and getting stuck in weather like this.

"Fish's probably begging for some sunscreen," I said.

"Your brain might be cooked, too." Pete was drinking off his beer, stuck it back between his legs.

We waited on throwing another line in till we didn't see that mad cackler rolling and flopping around in the water, trying to make further fools of us. The water splished-and-splashed on the bank real gentle. I, for sure, would've taken my shoes off and stuck my feet in, if I hadn't seen a million-and-a-half water moccasins sliding by in my lifetime. Jeffers was letting his line rest. I swear I think he closed his eyes, had himself a little peaceful moment, thinking about the way of the dolphin and such. Pete finally threw his line in the water again, saw his line tighten up for a second, then go slack.

"Probably a crab."

"Sure enough."

Jeffers finished his moment and checked his watch, wriggled his line for a second then reeled in some slack. What looked like a tidal wave, but was probably about a foot or so high, rolled outta nowhere. It was about a hundred yards off the bank, looking like a boat wake and coming right at us. A fin split the middle of the wake. That dolphin was coming back for seconds, but coming in real hot.

Pete looked at me. "What the hayell?"

"Got me," I said.

Me and Pete started backing up a bit. Just a few steps. Jeffers kept hanging his rod out there, all-peaceful. Wasn't giving a worried inch. Now the dolphin's head broke the water and he wasn't cackling no more. He was making a real guttural sound, more like a pig in heat or an asthmatic panther. That dolphin made a hundred yards quick and beached itself a couple feet in front of Pete, who'd slipped and flopped on his tail trying to scoot back. It looked right at him, eye-to-eye. I was thinking it might have some words for him. He had been a little disrespectful to the species. I guess I had too, though.

Huhhhh

HUHHHHHH

It was honking at Pete, making quite a racket, heaving and bellowing all donkey-like, still staring at Pete, who's pants were looking mighty wet for having just slipped on the river bank.

Sweet Mary. That thing spit the nastiest racket of phlegm right on him. The goo jingled when it hit Pete in the chest. He was wearing his favorite Wing House shirt, too. The bank of the river took on a smell that I don't guess I'll ever huff through my snout again. It was worse than I'd ever smelled at the Alligator Zoo-Park, and that's saying something. But that dolphin had just blessed poor Pete with the bottom of its stomach. Then the sonofabitch snatched the rest of Pete's beer and just kinda scooted on back into the water, sure and fast as he'd come out. He was gone.

"That just happen?" I asked. I shook my head a couple times real hard just in case I was having a little mini-trip.

"What a friendly thing," Jeffers said.

Pete looked over at Jeffers, mouth hanging open but only taking shallow breaths because of the stench. He very well could've been in shock.

"What you got there, Pete?" Jeffers nodded over at him.

Poor Pete looked down at his shirt and sat up a little, propping up from his elbows to his hands. The ball of goo toppled down from his chest to his belly, jingling in its flop. Pete picked at the goo with two fingers.

"My keys!" His mouth opened wider for a second, but he gagged a little.

Jeffers looked at his watch again. "Time to go."

Me and Jeffers each grabbed one of Pete's arms, me a little more careful than Jeffers to avoid the goo, and we picked him up, grabbed our stuff. I tried to catch a glance from Jeffers. He wouldn't look back at me. The walk back was quiet. The sea-birds were talking in the trees. Pete's smell probably reminded them it was getting close to dinner time. We still had time to get to Barney's place before he got hauled off. At Pete's, he changed shirts real quick and we grabbed some more booze from his fridge. He wasn't complaining about that. Pete was barely talking, just mumbling.

"Want me to drive?" I asked when we walked out to Pete's Caravan. It sat on eighteen-inch chrome-plated plastic hubcaps. They spun if you kicked them hard enough.

"Sure." Pete held out the keys. I pretended I didn't see them, just walked on around to the driver's door and let him unlock the van from the other side. I even let him put the keys in the ignition and turn them. The van cranked on the second try. We were on our way.

Pete had a radio in his van, but we kept it turned off. No other music or sound but nature could back up what we'd just taken in. We put the windows down, and it stayed quiet.

Barney wouldn't let us in the front door. I think we stunk. He said he was being watched and pointed to a car down the street. Pete waved and Jeffers elbowed him. He wiped off his elbow on the siding next to Barney's door. Barney didn't care. He wouldn't see his house for a while. He gave us a box of VHS tapes and I slipped him some cash on the other side of the box, so as to not let his friends down the street see.

We loaded the box up in the back and Jeffers and Pete started pilfering through those videotapes in the back while I drove.

"We got *Casper, Sisterhood of the Traveling Pants, Brother for Sale*." Pete was saying. "They're all loaded up in the cover! Bag a hash, some caps."

"Wait till we at least get down the street before you start unloading."

Barney'd been over to the goodwill.

"Sesame Street - Grover's Birthday, Jurassic Park II, these have got nothing in them."

"They may be for my boys. We watch a lot of movies. Barney knows that." I was getting a little antsy. "Let's get some of those mushrooms up here. I'm kinda hungry." I smiled back into the rearview. Pete ate him a handful before he passed them up my way. He had a kinda funny stomach sometimes, but I couldn't worry about him. He's a grown-ass man.

By the time we got to the house, Pete was fighting with the spare tire in the back of the van. Caps never did agree much with Pete. Jeffers and me usually saved those for our driving.

19

The last time I felt some grief was after Denny left me for the manager of the Craft Shack. I knew she'd been bringing home all these new patterns. She was making herself lots of new dresses and such. Learning new skills. Even made her a sexy witch dress for Halloween out of a fleece fabric with a bunch of candy corn and owls on it. I remember she was smelling like a werewolf after a night of trick-or-treating and gyrating. That was one of our last nights. Pretty soon after, I found a rainbow knitted bra in her purse, some number I hadn't had any pleasure in. Turns out it was getting used for somebody else. Somebody that could appreciate the time and expert use of knitting needles. I wrapped it around the vodka bottle in the freezer where I knew she'd find it. That was pretty close to being it for us. Really, I should've been wrapping her knittings around the bath salts. I thought she was having some peace for herself in the bathroom, but she was rolling up her issues of Women's Day instead of reading them. She was snorting those salts like a wild boar.

The end came when she accused me of cavorting with the cat. She stared at him a long time, then chased me outside and ate a good portion of the windshield wipers off the van. They were already broken anyway, but she put some good teeth marks in them. I threatened to drive off a few times before I finally put the van in reverse and rolled her off the hood. She lay there flailing and kicking, and I watched her from the street for a minute. Couldn't help but think she looked a lot like a bug. I'm not real sure what happened to the cat.

Truth was, it had been over for a while.

I picked the kids up from school, dropped them off at my momma's and tried to get disappeared for a minute. I needed to do some thinking, so I drove over to the Winn-Dixie parking lot. Back when it worked, I used to sit on the hood of my van a lot. Sometimes I'd open up the tailgate and sit on the back bumper if other folks were around. It was something to be proud of when it looked like I was losing everything else.

I went to grab Jeffers from work. It was a short drive. It felt funny to take the van when I usually walked or rode my bike. Jeffers wasn't surprised. I wasn't either.

"Long time coming, Jimmy." Jeffers never liked Denny, she'd tried to get down his pants a time or two. That's just who she was. I was never too concerned. As long as I knew the kids were mine.

"Want a ride?" I didn't need to ask but did. He was wrapping up anyway, putting his magic tricks in the closet.

"You holding?"

"A few beers. Half a joint." I imagined them waiting in the van, then remembered I had a beer in my hand and had a drink off it.

"Let's roll." He motioned with his hand. Somehow it seemed cool. The sky was red behind his hand. The trees were throwing shadows.

I handed Jeffers a beer, threw the shifter and dropped it into second, squeezed everything out of that worn out gear, then took my foot off the gas for a second and popped her into Drive, pushed the button on the end of the shifter and found Over Drive, waited out the lag and stomped the pedal to the floor. I was standing up.

"Woohoo!" I choked out, holding the last quarter inch of the joint in my mouth. My beer was in two fingers, the steering wheel in the other eight.

The Florida sky was starving and real thin. The toothpick clouds were like strips of speed bumps. There were no speed bumps on the blue asphalt superspeedway. I touched ninety and didn't back off the poor Windstar. The pine tree-lined highway was a blur of green and the cars I was weaving around were all screaming about the wheels on my van. They gestured in ways to tell me they were falling off. I felt the wobbling but knew it was the air pressure changing 'cause of my hyper speed. When I'd had enough to drink, the world stood still. I felt the motion of the van, a real smooth back-and-forth wobble, maybe even just a tilt of the big boat of a van in the water, moving with the swell of the asphalt ocean. I saw road ahead and a whole bunch of empty behind. Everything felt slow, even my memories.

Winn-Dixie's parking lot was littered with abandoned cars. The tow trucks didn't come for them because they knew there was no money in it. So the cars stayed. Security had a deer stand parked out there at the back of the lot. They kept folks from stealing the wheels off the empty cars. It was nice to not feel alone. I parked near an oak tree in its own island and tried to steal some privacy from the shadow.

We opened the back hatch and draped our legs over the bumper. Jeffers handed me a beer, we were getting near the end, but one of us could grab another suitcase from inside before they closed. It would keep security off our nuts if we bought something.

It seemed like the squeaky toy seagull sounds were piped in to remind me I was near the sea. The asphalt still smelled hot even though the day was cooling down. I bitched to Jeffers. He was just listening and drinking every time I stopped.

"Wasn't never real," I said.

"Nope."

"You think those seagulls are real?"

"I guess."

"But they never move." The seagulls stood real still. Their feathers blew in a light parking lot breeze. I had some snack crackers in my pocket. They were for one of the kids, but I forgot to give them to the boys. I tried to throw a couple out there in the parking lot, but they landed on top of a Cadillac, some ancient number, and a gaggle of seabirds jumped down on it like a feathery blizzard.

"Hey man. That's my car." I looked around till it felt like my head would roll right off my shoulders. Jeffers was looking too. There wasn't a soul around. The voice sounded like it came from my van.

"Don't start talking to me now. I already talked with crazy today." I patted the bumper and felt satisfied that maybe the talking was over.

"I ain't your car, man."

I pulled my hand off the bumper, looked at it a little wide-eyed.

"Up here." The voice was snapping fingers now. I looked up in the tree, some wreck of a man was draped over a branch in that oak. Laying flat with his head resting on his hands.

I was squinting my eyes real tight in the twilight. "What the hell you doing up there?"

"Same thing you're doing. Pondering." He had a cooler up in that tree, hanging by a rope. Just laying up there on that branch drinking. "Living chased me up this here tree. I intend on staying a while."

"You sleep up there?"

"Not yet."

"You real?" Jeffers asked. That weed was pretty good. The beer was better.

"Far as I can tell." He sat up a little on the branch. "Why you asking?"

"It's twilight. A man can get to seeing things." Jeffers never really looked up. Don't know that he had even seen the man up there yet.

"Nothing's real nohow." Here we were listening to the trees.

"Not with women, they never are," I muttered. The first time I ever hung out with Denny, I set her hair on fire. Jeffers and me called her the burning bush ever since. She said she thought it was funny. She was a liar. "How'd you get up that tree?" I was more into the logistics. There weren't any low branches.

"Does it matter? I'm here 'cause I'm here."

The red, orange, and purple of twilight turned the spaces between branches into stained glass, burning up, but not burning out. I couldn't see the man's face or features. The warm light from behind set the tree on fire, but I was all toast up in my head. The beer didn't help settle me. I was restless and didn't have no time for listening to somebody else's problems. Especially no man in a tree. Jeffers always had time to listen. He took his shoes off and stood up on the hood. I got up and tried to catch one of the seagulls off the hood of the Cadillac. I was trying to see if was real or a decoy. I swear one of those birds asked me if I was real.

They flew up together.

When I turned around and looked, that man was talking and Jeffers was looking at the ground.

"I'm going for more beer," I called back. They weren't hearing me.

The gulls laughed at me from on top of the light posts when I walked through the parking lot. I wanted to be their friend, but they heckled me like mad. They knew I'd had a rough go of it. They said everything in unison. A chorus of cackling, prodding, and picking. Their gray faces hid behind ruffled feathers so that I couldn't tell them apart from one another. I asked them how they got lost, so far from the water, and they flew away. No creature likes having its errors pointed out.

I was kinda pissed at Jeffers when I got back. I'd brought him over here to listen to me bitch, and all he did was listen to a man in a tree and drink all my beer. I even had to buy more. But I was happy to see that Cadillac, with all its birds, and the man in the tree gone. The sun had dropped out and the tree wasn't on fire anymore.

"Where'd your new buddy go?"

"Hmm?" Jeffers was looking at his can. It was pinched in on the sides from him turning it round and round. I took the old beat-up one and gave him a new beer from the fresh box.

"Home, I guess?" He had me answering my own questions.

We sat there quiet for a while.

"Jimmy. You believe in real magic?"

"What you meaning by real?"

"I don't know. I mean." Jeffers was breathing through his mouth. "We were always trying to fool people. I do it at the park. People's always asking me to do the trick again so they can figure it out."

He stood up and walked under the tree, looked up. "What if there weren't no figuring? Making it real, *Mag-ni-fi-cent*."

"You gonna make Denny disappear?" I was downright hopeful.

"Jimmy, you can't take a thing serious." He crossed his arms. "I'm talking about doing things hadn't been done before and you can't get your mind off a woman's been done plenty."

I threw a full beer at Jeffers. Wasn't really pissed. Just a little. But he was right, as always. Denny wasn't the best-looking woman I'd ever been with, but I loved her heart. She was gone by the time I got back. Got a phone call from Sheriff Chuck a little bit later asking if it was normal for her to walk around the middle of the highway wearing a bed sheet with eyes cut out of it. I gave him the phone number to the Craft Shack from the yellow pages. The trailer was a wreck. It took me a couple days to get it back to looking like normal.

20

There were two boats at the Alligator Zoo-Park, and one of them worked. Mr. Cotter never minded us taking one out just as long as he got him some fish out of it. He really didn't mind anything Jeffers wanted to do so long as the people kept coming through the gates of the Alligator Zoo-Park to see the magic show. Jeffers put the place up in lights. Folks started coming from all over. Mr. Cotter started driving him a German car painted up like a gator.

Like the one boat, other things around the park stopped working. The mermaid tank backed up a couple times with swamp grass and otter droppings. The glass got real foggy and it got hard to see the show. The girls' flips and such were swirling with mud and bubbles. Nobody much was bothered. The people had stopped going to the mermaid shows anyway. The snake warmers and the baby tanks had their lights go out. Mr. Cotter just had Judd let them loose in the wild. They lived around there anyhow. Wasn't a big deal. The main den was all that mattered. The folks lined the bleachers and gobbled up hot dogs and waited to watch the man work his miracles. People were talking a lot. I listened to them.

I heard he re-grew an arm.

He got a demon out from a woman. Made some birds go crazy at the froyo.

He's got him a whole army of gators he's puttin' together, gonna help him run for office.

More of the park mattered to Judd. Things weren't getting lost on him. Ever since his show got moved to an opening act, he'd been more than a little frustrated. For a long time it seemed like he was going to swallow it and move on along, but then the Game Warden started lurking around. I even saw Judd out talking to him at the Chili's one night when I was trying to sneak in a two-for on some gin and tonics.

Jeffers started asking me to tell him anytime I saw anything funny like that, and I did. Jeffers was making something. He built something big where nothing much was. I had a lot of respect for him. I'd helped him make it.

We rounded up about as much booze as we could fit on the boat and then realized we didn't have the fishing gear. I was surprised the thing ended up floating us.

We had to sneak Miriam in without Mr. Cotter seeing her since she had gone out on disability and such. He wasn't a big fan of hers. So when the Alligator Zoo-Park had shut down for Sunday, we walked through the park and listened to the gators bellow. They huffed and honked and generally just sounded like they were burping, and the birds sat around watching us suspiciously. They didn't want to be putting on any type of show, and the sight of Jeffers made them think they might have to get to work. They all watched Jeffers like he was the boss.

Pete and Andy came along and Andy pushed a dolly with all the booze, a couple-three jugs of Carlo and a few suitcases of Bud.

The tires on that thing damn near went flat and it kept leaning to one side. Probably wasn't blown up in the first place.

"How long you supposing we're gonna be out here?" Pete was counting the cases.

"As long as it takes to get us some dinner." I was answering for Jeffers. He was walking along with Miriam pointing out anything new he thought she might not have seen yet since she left.

"Pull over a second, Andy." I was thirsty. Grabbed me a beer and pulled out a couple for anybody else that was needing one. We kept on rolling, walking toward the dock and the cans started spilling out the side of the case. They sputtered after hitting the ground and got all dinged up. They were cold too, so we drank them up—just popped the tabs and shot-gunned them right there. Thought we were off to a good start, 'cause I started feeling a buzz shortly after.

The river was narrow there. Really, it was just a creek off the St. Johns. It was low tide and smelled like a possum crapped on a napkin and handed it to you. All of those critters were dying out of water and we got to smell them. When it was quiet enough, which was never, the marsh made these bubbling and hissing sounds, with all the mud breathing and letting all its gas out for us to smell. I could throw a rock from one side of the creek to the other, and did a couple times, trying to hit those birds and the occasional gator camping out cooling his belly on some marsh mud. It was hard to throw the shells, though. They were the sharp oyster shells all stuck together and mudded up stinking.

The dock was old and creaked a lot, especially with the dolly whomping along on one good wheel. We damn near lost all the booze over the side. But the mud was exposed at slack tide, so my worry went away kinda quick. It wouldn't be hard to get back long as some gator didn't snatch it and get his teeth all purple. We'd given Lazarus's big-old-gator self some wine more than a couple times. He liked it good enough, usually limped along asking for more. He'd just lie there and stick his mouth open, let us glug a little down his gullet. His tongue would get all purple and people would ask about his teeth. It was hard to explain off, so we laid off boozing with him. He was a rowdy drunk.

Both boats looked the same and neither of them had a name painted on. They were tied-up to the dock and looked all peaceful and boring. They had names once a long time ago, but they were relics and the Florida sun cooked the names off the same as it did everything else. Jeffers jumped on the first one and tried cranking it. Nothing happened. He climbed on the second one and it cranked first try.

"It's that one," Andy said, and folks just kinda looked at him.

The boats had big flat yellow pontoons and a plastic top propped on red columns. There were these porthole-looking windows along the top that nobody had ever been tall enough to look through. The whole thing looked like an antique school bus bobbing along and trying to go nowhere in particular. The bottom was see-through and it stretched between the pontoons and there were a few rows of hard plastic seats on either side of the aisle. They were cracked and faded and the plastic peeled when you scratched them with a fingernail. I watched my step real-careful following Jeffers, then scratched "Jimmy wuz here" on one of the seat backs. I gave myself a second before I looked down. Nothing was trippier than climbing on that boat and looking at all the junk underneath, fishes coming up, looking at us like we was out of place. I made faces at them and realized they couldn't care less. I did it again, anyway.

"Lemme hand you all this shit," Pete was saying, wearing his Wing House shirt, and me hoping it'd been washed. I put my beer down on one of the seats and took the cases of beer as he handed them over. I put them all toward the back and made sure to lay the booze out flat so it wouldn't go overboard. Pete climbed on. and Andy tried to give Miriam a hand over the side, but she wouldn't take it.

"We ready?" Jeffers was asking.

Andy walked down the dock a little, to the back of the boat. "Yep. Lemme get these lines." He let it loose, then made his way to the front, held the line and jumped on. Jeffers moved the throttle and tried to put the boat in gear. The gears ground and jerked, but nothing happened. The boat didn't move. The mud swirled through the glass bottom and I watched it. Glass wasn't supposed to get that close to the water.

"How'd we sink a pontoon?" He moved the throttle back and forth and the motor started sputtering mud. Then he cut it. "Lemme get a beer." I brought him one from the back. "Jimmy, we can't keep all the beer back there."

"Don't matter, Jeffers." I handed it to him. "We aren't moving either way. Front's bogged down, too. Slack tide."

"We got to wait it out."

"We can do that."

We must have sat on the boat the better part of two hours to get out of dead-low. Not much breeze was blowing through and we thought about jumping in a couple times but weren't drunk enough to blow off the gators watching us. Miriam polished off a jug and we moved through the second case of Bud. We crunched up the empties and threw them at the gators. Finally, the front end started trying to float again. We spread out the booze in seats around the boat like the cases were tourists, might've even started talking to them a little. We spread out too and shouted at each other over the engine once Jeffers fired it again. Didn't have to untie the lines again, because we forgot to tie them back down once we started really feeling the booze. Jeffers had us moving down the creek and I watched the sea birds turning their heads real startled-like as they picked us up coming along. Every one of them flew off their branches when our two-stroke bus-boat got close enough. Then the water opened up and we were out into the river. It was a good three miles across, looked enough like an ocean that it might as well have been one. The pontoon didn't like the chop as much as it did the calm in the coves. Jeffers pulled it into a bank of trees and little inlet that stuck out a ways into the water. It looked like the trees were growing out of the lake. It was calm enough.

"I've got smoke." I'd brought a little baggy with a nugget and Miriam said she was game. I was real careful when I slipped off the boat to keep the lighter and the one-hitter over my head and out of the water. The bottom was shallow and we walked up under the glass between the pontoons.

"Looks real weird from the other side, don't it?" Miriam and me could see bodies and faces, but everything was wonky in a way. Just color and shape and real blurry. Looking up was different than looking down. I handed her the one-hitter and she took a toke, went under water for a second and snorkeled the smoke out.

The smoke got trapped down there between the pontoons, and I sucked in as much of it as I could. Miriam handed me the one-hitter and I gave it a go. The water lapped at the pontoons with a hollow tap. More light glowed from the ends of the boat than came down through the glass and everything looked yellow. Lines of light reflected on our faces like electricity, but so much slower.

"Jimmy, you think it's ever going to be enough?" Her eyes were squinty, but she was serious looking.

"The weed?" I coughed.

"Nah, Jimmy. She was treading water with her arms, long and slender, but standing on the bottom just like me. I figured I didn't make such a pretty picture, myself. "The people. The, the, what's the word? The *following*." Miriam looked sad. Sad, but pretty. Maybe there was always a dark edge on her cloud—that rim of shadow that floats off along the edges of puffy white. "There is no moment. You know what I'm saying?" I nodded but had no clue. I tried to tread the water like her. Thankfully I had enough brains left to keep the smoke above the surface. Dipped my chin in and blew some bubbles. "You got spit chin, Jimmy." I thought about it later, and she was right. She had the words, but I didn't have the wits for it. Miriam was always smarter than me, but she was a little off too. There was a moment. Just not for her and me. There was always the moment of total disbelief of the crowd—the followers. There was the moment when they couldn't believe what they saw, the moment just before they totally believed in Jeffers.

I lit up again and dipped under water, breathed out through my nose and made a smoky cloud on top. It spread out and looked heavy but kept on floating. Miriam chased it around, sucking like a dustbuster. I coughed a little and we were running out of air for sure. The space started to feel hot.

"You good?"

"I'm good."

We kinda bobbed back out from under the boat. Andy and Jeffers were waiting.

"My turn." Andy held out his hand for the one-hitter.

"You're not even going to offer to help a man aboard?" I started laughing, but Andy was already in the water. Pete came over too and flopped down.

"You almost got the lighter wet." Nobody really cared. It was just something to say. My mind was on a billion other things, like counting branches in the trees and only getting to five, over and over again. Me and Miriam climbed up in the boat. I laid down flat on my face and pressed it against the glass-bottom, looked down at the tops of their heads and the smoky water and tried to see how long I could go without blinking. The air was cooler now and the sun was dimming. I could feel the clouds cover us up. I might've nearly gone to sleep with my eyes open if Miriam wouldn't have started stomping on the glass and they wouldn't have splashed and tramped out from under us. The boat was rocking.

Miriam was yelling something, lots of words I couldn't tell. She pounded the glass below with her fists. I just laid there watching things move in slow motion. The boat spit them out both ends, and I realized I needed to hop up. I went to the front and helped Pete out, Miriam was helping Andy out of the water and up on the boat.

She pointed out to the middle of the river. Miriam was yelling.

"Waterspout!"

I turned and saw that funnel looking like a snake, climbing and spinning from the water up to the darkest cloud the sky could muster. It was near purple-colored in the middle of the river. It definitely wasn't far enough away to make anybody comfortable. Me and Miriam, Pete and Andy, huddled in a fright. Then I checked the console and thank goodness the keys were in the ignition, but something else was missing.

"Oh shit!" I scrambled over to the edge of the boat on my knees, looking up under the pontoons.

"Jeffers!"

But he wasn't around the boat.

In the shallows and walking further out, was my friend. It looked like he wanted to catch that spout. He kept wading out, elbows held up above the surface like he was dancing, and that funnel kept creeping closer to him. The water was shimmying, light bouncing off little peaks and troughs, but it kept neat and tidy around Jeffers. I swear we were watching a ghost out there in the river. The St. Johns for-sure wasn't the cleanest. It was dark water. But, it looked like a billion little crystals when the dark clouds let that little stream of light come down to Jeffers. It might've been lightning, I don't know. He was the only light thing out there. It was downright spooky. Jeffers reached out to the waterspout with both hands and it looked like it scooted right up to him. He grabbed it like a hi there, how are you? and I swear, as soon as he touched it, that thing fell apart. Whole bunch of water came down in a wall. Just broke right on Jeffers and we couldn't see him anymore. Bunches a fish came splashing down around him. I might've even seen the dolphin that stole Pete's beer come flopping out with a *aeeaeeaeeeeee*. Of course, out of all that water and such came Jeffers, walking. Walked on out to the shallows where we were all still standing around on the boat maybe having peed our pants.

"Let's move the boat over there," he said, and pointed over to the mess of fish and life in general flopping out on the water, celebrating having dropped back to earth and not spinning 'round in circles no more. "We'll get us some fish!"

And man, we caught buckets. We'd throw a line in and catch a fish and a bigger fish would snatch that fish and a bigger one yet would jump on to get them a little bit of the other fish and we'd end up with a big old fish on the line. It was wearing out my arms hauling in those honkers. We were cooked after a bit and finally called it. Never seen so many fish as we had piled up on the boat. We drank all the beer and started in on Miriam's last bottle of Carlo. The smell of the fish on the boat got to Pete and he started spraying purple here and there. We left him at the back of the boat and I dropped beer cans over the front to watch them float under the glass-bottom all the way out the back. Sometimes, they'd get caught by the motor, but it was spinning fast enough not to foul the prop.

We pulled the boat up close to the dock, Andy jumped and tied it off. Nobody else much had any legs left after spending so much time with that smell. Mr. Cotter was waiting on the dock and didn't seem too pleased at catching sight of Miriam. But Jeffers gave him a whole mess of those fish and the old cat couldn't stop grinning. Left us all be and rolled his cooler on home to his woman—maybe Aunt Becky.

21

Maybe it was the city-boy with the ear, or the papers talking about Jeffers' new arm, but people were definitely mumbling about the happenings and Jeffers' magic shows.

Mr. Cotter put in a new tap for beer at the snack bar and shut down the mermaids. The Alligator Zoo-Park was pulling folks from as far away as Georgia, maybe even the panhandle. Jeffers the Magnificent was the ticket. So when Jeffers told Mr. Cotter that his next big trick wasn't going to be at the Alligator Zoo-Park, I figure he was mighty pissed. Mr. Cotter might've been ready to make Jeffers disappear.

Jeffers had me and Miriam walk around putting up fliers. I guess nearly every light pole in the county—for sure every one of those in the park—had a picture of Jeffers doing magic on it. Miriam drew up every single one of them fliers her ownself. There were pictures in colored pencils of Jeffers hanging over some big gator's teeth and there was a picture of Jeffers walking across a bunch of gators' backs. It kinda looked like he was tap dancing. There was even one of an alligator wearing a top hat waving a wand. I really liked that one a whole lot. They all said things like "Jeffers The Magnificent" or "WOW." She really was into those drawings. Jeffers said she'd been up all night working on them. Wore out a whole set of pencils and got her hands to cramping. That explained to me how some of the later pictures were in pinks and purples. But she wanted him to be known, appreciated.

We drove all over trying to figure out where to put on the next show. Spent a whole afternoon and drank a suitcase of beer just looking at spots and talking and kinda figuring they just weren't right. We wrapped up in time to try seeing my boys play some ball over at the Dixie League lot. Me and Jeffers parked behind the centerfield fence and polished off our last couple beers watching the boys drop pop flies. Then we cruised on over to the stands and saw my momma.

"You boys are stinking."

"We've been working, Momma. What kind of greeting's that, anyhow?" I saw her pocket a flask. Slipped it right out of her rolled up issue of *The Star*.

"Boys are 0-for-6."

"Sounds about right."

The evening smelled like dirt and peanuts. Jeffers grabbed us a couple tiny paper cups of co-cola and it dawned on me.

"Jeffers, *this* is your spot." I looked out over the ballfield—at all the flies lighting up flittering in the big spotlights. The bleachers hugged around the fence.

"You think?"

"I do. Just got to figure out what the trick's going to be."

The headlights covered every inch of street for miles around the Dixie League fields. Looked like daytime except for the moon being out.

Me and Jeffers got there real early, prepping and such. Folks were kind enough to let us use the concession stand and Miriam was pouring co-cola in just about every little waxy cup she could find, selling them and making rent. The bleachers filled up by dusk and people lined the outfield fence a few deep. Near everybody had an animal on a string. Dogs and cats were yanking on chains and talking about this and that. Trying to get a bite or a sniff of each other. We were too busy to take much notice.

Jeffers gave me a nod up in the score-keeping booth and I got on the microphone. I'd been thinking a whole lot about my flopping through life. Kinda threatening nothingness at just about every bend and turn. In that moment, I felt pretty good about things. It was all looking and feeling pretty real.

"Ladies and Gentlemen. *Jeffers the Mag-ni-fi-cent!*" I looked off to the side. "I say that right?" Folks clapped a little. Mostly just kept talking. Jeffers just nodded. Walked out and got started down on the field. He waved his arms for people to cool down a second.

"For this one, I'm going to need me a volunteer from the crowd." There was some grumbling coming out from the people, some dogs yipping here and there, but a little girl came running out on the field with a raccoon on a rainbow-colored shoestring. She must've been about six or seven. Every time that raccoon humped and hustled along, that string would fling up a little bit and look like a promise. The crowd started cheering.

Jeffers pulled him out a pack of cards from his pocket. He wanted to start off the night kinda small. Move on to the bigger stuff, maybe catch a bullet or cut somebody in half.

"Going to need you to pick one of these here cards from your pocket." He handed the little girl a marker. "You know how to write your name?" She shook her head and looked real confused.

"My raccoon here, Bobby, he's got him a bad toe." She pointed down and was right. I saw him favoring it a little bit when he was shuffling up to Jeffers on that string.

Jeffers looked straight at me, a little thrown off with that, but he left the marker in her hand.

"You want to just put your initials on the card? You know your letters?" She shook her head again.

We cain't hear you real good! Somebody was yelling from the crowd. Jeffers'd been trying to be loud, but I could tell he didn't want to scare that little girl or her raccoon, neither.

"What's your name, then?" Jeffers asked her, reaching for that marker. "I'll go on and write it on there for you."

That girl was still looking confused.

"When you gonna start the healing?" She reached down and gave Bobby some scratches. "He's been hurting." Raccoon looked to me like he was doing alright. Kinda looked wily, maybe had some rabies or something light like that.

Jeffers looked down at her. "Honey, this here's a magic show."

Little girl's eyes started getting all twinkly like my boys' did when they were telling the cat it was the best cat in the whole wide world, and me, standing there, holding a tire iron.

With that the crowd got a little rowdy. A couple bottles got tossed over the fence and Jeffers started yelling, "Whoa! Whoa!" and put himself in front of that little girl. I walked down the steps out of the booth. It was looking like there might have to be some crowd control. I had Jeffers' keys and I started walking toward the NAILR.

Folks started chanting.

Healin'! Healin'! Healin'!

People were wanting Jeffers to fix their pets. We'd somehow missed it. They weren't looking for no magic show, they were looking for miracles.

"STOP!" Jeffers waved his hands. The whole place got silent. I stopped, too, and watched, keys in the door to the NAILR still jangling and swinging back-and-forth. Jeffers turned back to Bobby and the girl. He crouched and sat down. That coon started flopping every-which-way when Jeffers grabbed him, but eventually he put Bobby in his lap. The girl stood between him and the crowd. Folks were leaning in, some climbed up the fence a little. Everybody was angling for a view.

"Aw, *Bobby!*" That girl was getting sad watching Jeffers wrastling with her pet and it was jabbering up a storm, too. Wasn't a dog, I knew that, but some folks just couldn't get over how cuddly those pudgy raccoons looked after they'd been snacking on their garbage for about a year or so.

"Hold still!" I could hear Jeffers getting frustrated. His patience was tending to run out a little quick. He was tired and his plans had gotten changed on him. Instead of sawing some good-looking woman in half, he was trying to heal a raccoon.

Little girl was crying pretty good now, "You hurting him?"

He hurting Bobby?

He's out there hurting Bobby!

Sicko!

People were getting restless. They started moving towards the gaps in the fence, jimmying with the gates and such.

Folks would swear they saw a flash of light, maybe even a popping sound come off the field. A couple of local papers said things about angels singing or some kinda angelic voice crying out. I know that's when that coon let out a squeal and a whistle like I've never heard before or since and that little girl cried out, "*Bobby!*"

Everybody got a real treat when that raccoon jumped out of Jeffers' lap, gimpy toes good as new, and started running around the field all crazed. What I saw was Jeffers flopped over passed out.

Papers talked about some loony driving over the little league field fence in a minivan with folks jumping out of the way. Drove out on the field and kidnapped him some Jeffers. Truth was, I saw them people getting all their pets ready for some healing and a passed-out Jeffers that wasn't going to be able to take it. Crowd was ready to mob, and I had to get him out of there. So I did. I cranked up the NAILR and I hit the horn, drove right on through that crowd of puppy dogs and cats and people jumping out of the way when I ran right over that fence and onto the field. I felt real bad about Bobby, I didn't know how fast he was going to be with his new toes and I felt like it was pretty quick and painless when I ran him over. Papers didn't like that, either. Newly healed raccoon's life cut short by minivan with a nice picture of Bobby smiling in some kinda Olan Mills-looking photo. I threw Jeffers in the back and left, right on back out the way I came. People were in a frenzy. Somebody threw a ferret at the van, somebody else threw a cat— that's what I was thinking it was anyway. I watched them go pick it up again in the side mirror. We got chased for a block or so. Lots of folks at first, but running's hard, and about a block or so later it was just Miriam. I stopped and let her in and we drove on.

"Takes a lot out of him, don't it?" Miriam was looking back at passed out Jeffers there sprawling in the back of the van.

"Think so."

22

F olks in the park were always looking for a miracle. Some easy way to cure their ills. They wanted some homegrown son that could fix them. When they couldn't find that wonderboy, or he couldn't be the one to do it, they turned on him just as fast as they got excited for the fix.

Jeffers had an audience. It was the most satisfied and uncomfortable I'd ever seen the man. He was making magic and pleasing people, but I swear it made him weary. Jeffers got to being removed from things, and more than a little snappy. Working with Lazarus and the gators and upping his tricks was wearing him out. He was turning into a gator, moved real fast and hard, then wore out quick from his cold blood. He had about a billion little cuts and scrapes on his hands and his arms. Even his "new arm" wasn't looking fresh. Crowds came out from town to see him at work, making seabirds disappear and then reappear out of a gator's mouth, cutting gators in two and making them whole again, doing the rings while they were on fire and having a gator jump through them. It all added up and wore him pure out. The crowds had built. They didn't just start big. Jeffers put on a show near every single day. When things started looking miracle-like, that's when the mobs of folks started coming.

The believers were the most spooky. People got downright attached. There were folks that wouldn't let him go. I swear I saw him get offered a baby or two. Somehow, those people just couldn't see anybody doing better for the kids. Instead, he'd sign his name on a baby. Next best thing for them. I'd watch those folks driving right over to the tattoo parlor. There were baby's around town with Jeffers' name on their hinds real permanent.

Miriam started feeling a little spooked. Maybe a little bit jealous too. It must've been tough being with Jeffers and all, sharing your man with everybody else thinking they had him, too. Miriam told me about some of those feelings.

I know I got to feeling left behind, my ownself.

They wanted Jeffers, physically, mentally, they wanted pieces of him, something for them to own and hold just for them, but they still wanted him on the stage, too. They wanted to be there to witness him in his magnificence and have the right to say that they had seen him. I'm not sure he wanted greatness, but I think he always knew it was going to happen with the skills he had. Lots of folks found it easy to write off the work he had to put into his shows by saying that he was "born with it." I remembered the hours and the time spent locked up in his room. For growing up with nothing, he sure did find a bunch of something, especially attention.

Jeffers was getting dressed up. The fanciest thing he had was a decent uniform from the Alligator Zoo-Park. Think it was a jumper, one of those one-piece deals in an unstained khaki color. Most everything else he owned had plenty of stains. We were running through the tricks like we always did. I wasn't much of an assistant,

more just an ear to hear, and a tester for things that needed test-
ing. Jeffers could walk me through a trick and I'd let him know if I
thought it would do what he was wanting. He would get all itchy
for finding what he was looking for. Only time I ever felt that way
was when I cleaned the catbox. I would pretend I was sifting for
gold. Only things Denny really left me with was the kids and the
cat. The cat found its way down Chubby's throat. That's how things
went for me, mostly, thinking I'm finding gold when really all I
was doing was shaking dirt off some turds. Every now and then,
I'd find a new trick and try and tell Jeffers about it, show it off, but
he'd already figured out a better way, some way I couldn't have
figured. I never much minded letting Jeffers be the show. I knew
for sure that it couldn't have been me. It just wasn't for me to be.

But Jeffers was getting worn down from being in that spotlight.
He found himself being about as public as a mayor.

I was taking Jeffers up on a ride over to the Craft Shack so I could
get some money from Denny. She got herself hired over there with
the dude that'd been managing her hide for a minute and finally
agreed to spot me some cash for eating the windshield wipers. She
knew it wasn't her best behavior. Didn't even need the judge to
tell her. But I was feeling a little mopey and thought it might pick
me up to see her working. Jeffers was wanting to go anyhow. It was
picture day at the Alligator Zoo-Park, and he needed to pick up
some frames with wild animals all over them to put the pictures
in once they got them back from the one-hour photo.

It was a pretty big day in the parking lot. The gun show was at the
Moroccan Shrine. If I had enough cash for a ticket and a two-for-

one at Chili's, I would do both. But I checked, and funds were short. I knew I wasn't going to get much out of Denny. Never had.

The Craft Shack was home to the unhappiest, most generally miserable people on the planet. There was yarn for days and I swear it smelled like I got a cinnamon broom stuck up my nose the second the doors slid open. Not a soul in site had hopped in bed with a warm body or hoped for a happy ending in a couple decades, that was for sure. Except Denny, of course. She was working the sewing section and had a man's hand on her giant ass while she measured off some yarn. Man looked like St. Nick and it only made sense because they were so busy celebrating Christmas all the time. I knew she was hiding some Reese's under the desk.

"How can I help *you*?" She was acting all professional, like some kinda professional hoochie.

"Let me get one of them peanut butter cups."

"I can tell you where to get a whole heap of go fuck yourself." She always made things sound so sweet and every word she burped out smelled like vodka.

"You want me to call security, baby?" St. Nick was having a little trouble wiggling his hefty hand out the back pocket of her Old Navy denim.

"You going to go grab Prancer, Dancer, and the whole rest a them eight tiny reindeer?" He looked at me like he didn't get the joke. I knew Jeffers would've got it, but he was off looking at custom frames for fifty-percent off. "You the manager?"

"I am."

"I want to file a complaint about your employee here. Ate my windshield wipers right off my van." He was still working on getting his hand back out of that pocket trying to chomp on it.

"Here's your money, Jimmy." She reached down to grab her purse, Santa still attached. Pulled out a little wad of ones and tossed it at me. I knew it wasn't much. Didn't bother counting.

"And a Reese's." Kinda felt like a stick-up, but I wanted what was owed. I bought so many peanut butter cups and never got one.

She reached under the table and popped up, tossed a Reese's at me. I didn't have to duck or shimmy to get outta the way. She was always a bad aim, whether it was a shoe, a cat, or a bottle she was throwing. So I walked away, left them to untangle, and went looking around the floor for that Reese's. Didn't matter which aisle it landed on or how scuffed it got, I was going to eat that thing. Found it rolled up next to a magic snowman display—tipped his hat and sang a little—and I worked on the crinkled edges of the milk chocolate while I poked around the aisles looking for Jeffers.

Found him over a couple more aisles still staring at a wall full of frames.

"You know what size?" I said to him. He didn't even look up.

"Think so." He was staring at a picture with the sample photo in it. Some happy looking family prancing on a lawn with targets on them with a frame around it saying "Home on the Range." I picked up a frame with a whole bundle of jungle cats on it saying "Just Purrrfect."

"I kinda like this one." I was holding up the jungle cats, being for real.

"You should get it." He didn't give it a glance.

"Don't have no pictures." But he knew that.

"I'm going to go grab a buggy." Jeffers walked off and left me looking at frames I didn't have any interest in. Some old woman came buzzing down the lane trying to take my toes off with her buggy without even a nod. Jeffers came back around.

"Here we go." Found him a frame with a big green gator on it, wrapping its tail around the whole thing. Said "See ya later!" across the top.

"Man. That's just about right, isn't it?" So we started dumping them in the buggy. Must've got like seventeen of those things. They were cute. I felt good 'cause it was my idea. We cruised on through the checkout line with the beep-beep-beeps and some lady asking, "That all?" real angered.

"How are you today?" I said.

Denny must've told all these folks some stories. I wanted to set them straight, tell them all that I was nothing but good to her. First time I got a little sad and lonely thinking about things. But that was what the craft store was for, anyhow. Felt a whole lot better when I got out to the van, drank a beer or two in the parking lot and watched them folks peering at us through the glass.

"Got everything you were needing?"

"Guess so." I watched the cashier lady pressed up against the window staring while we drove outta the lot. Could've swore she was saying, "help," but realized pretty quick she was just standing under the *Help Wanted* sign.

I ate a cap and cranked the radio to get us a little mariachi. Some song about love and things that didn't matter much. I just knew it was about love 'cause of all the moaning and crooning. Love sure would make a man do strange things. The moaning wasn't the worst of it. But listening to another man do it wasn't making me feel much better in my head. All I could imagine was that little man in the radio was Santa. I let the radio wind down a little bit then switched it over to the sports radio.

...and Jeffers the Magnificent! Tuesdays are two for one on adult admission. Kids drink free!

"You can turn it off, Jimmy." Jeffers wasn't liking the new commercial. Things had been getting pretty big for Mr. Cotter. He was feeling mighty, putting up commercials and such. I could've swore I saw Jeffers shrinking in the driver seat. I switched it back over to the mariachi station and watched a row of orange road cones lift off like rocket ships as my mushrooms started kicking in. Neither one of us were going to have the ride or the peace we were wanting. But I was pretty sure I wasn't feeling as much heat as Jeffers. World wasn't sitting on my shoulders, Denny sure as hell wasn't, either. I could listen to the little man croon and hump a note or two on his trumpet without getting too worked up.

We rolled into the Alligator Zoo-Park parking lot just in time to see Judd finish taking a leak in a freshly potted palm. He zipped himself up and walked back in the park, slicking his hair with a hand I wouldn't shake if it was trying to save me from drowning. Before I could think too hard about why he wasn't using the men's room, I saw Mr. Cotter come outta there with a gator in a mermaid outfit, then a mermaid walking another gator on a leash. That one had on a mountain of lipstick and got all dressed up like a china doll. Guess he was diversifying the show again.

"Jeffers, what y'all doing to these gators?" I was asking while we got out of the van and Jeffers grabbed the bag with the frames. We started walking in past the mermaid tank. A woman with a camera was telling folks to yank the gators this way and that. Propping them up on things, Duck taping umbrellas in their claws and making them sit around a table all set up with tea cups and a table cloth.

"They're getting dressed up for the pictures. Mr. Cotter's looking for something more professional. Feels like it'll keep the show in the park."

"I guess I'd bite somebody's hand off if they dressed me up like that." The tea party gators were grunting and generally sounding more than a little pissy.

"They got me a suit I've got to wear."

"Sounds fancy. They're dressing you like a real magician?" He didn't bother to answer. We walked up to the main tank. Down in the den, they'd put together a whole city's worth of buildings out of cardboard boxes.

"Model of Jacksonville, there." Jeffers was pointing. "I have to protect it from Lazarus."

"Looks like a whole bunch of paper cuts to me." It was pretty fancy. I didn't like to let on. Jeffers handed me the bag of frames and walked back over to the photographer lady. She sent him to the bathroom for getting made up. I looked down in the den and Lazarus looked bored as all get-out. He snorted every now and then but didn't make much fuss out of the ordinary. Just kinda sniffed on the cardboard a little. Jeffers came back a minute later with the photographer lady. Sonofabitch was wearing a gorilla costume. Judd was trailing behind them with a model airplane hanging off a fishing pole.

"What you think, Jimmy?" that gorilla said to me.

"I give up on thinking."

The photographer lady started calling out, "Who's going to powder the alligator?"

"They're going to put makeup on Lazarus?" Jeffers didn't answer me, though. I might as well've been one of them cardboard buildings. Jeffers climbed down in the den and I swear Lazarus wasn't much for the gorilla costume. I got it, then. They wanted something grand. This was it. King Kong and Godzilla, Jeffers and Lazarus. Some poor mermaid got down there and put a little powder on Lazarus. Made him less shiny. Looked good for the camera. But old Lazarus had things he wanted to do, and it wasn't to wreck a cardboard city and eat a Jeffers gorilla. He snatched that powder poof right outta that mermaid's hand and ate it up. Started gagging like I'd never seen a gator do. She might've lost a finger, but Lazarus wasn't going to get to enjoy it. Gator started shooting powder out his nose like a fire extinguisher and whipping that whole goddam cardboard city down with his tail in a couple swoops.

"Anybody got a cup of water?" Jeffers yelled. He looked straight at me.

I felt all seized up. My beer brain had me planted.

Then Lazarus rolled down the bank and into the lazy river. A minute later he was floating on his back, looking dead as could be.

"You killed my gator!" Mr. Cotter was yelling at that mermaid. She was grabbing her finger and running toward the exit, couldn't care less what he was saying. Some other folks were rushing along with her. It was a mess.

Jeffers was all arms, gorilla-hustling down the bank, grabbed Lazarus by the tail and got to pulling him up the muddy slope.

"Anybody help?" Jeffers was shouting through that gorilla mask all muffled. But nobody did. He was all on his own, but he wasn't one to give up on a dead gator, especially Lazarus. He pulled and pulled till he got that big old gator up on dry land, jumped on his back and started bouncing on him. Lazarus was puffing some more. Looked like he was smoking. Jeffers got off his back and looked at his snout, eye to eye, gorilla to gator. Pulled his mouth open with one furry arm and reached down in the gator's gullet with the other. He pulled him out a poof, then got back to bouncing on Lazarus' back.

The rumbling grunt that came out of Lazarus was like life coming back with a thunder. I never did see a gator look so much like Denny. Last thing he choked up was that finger.

That photographer woman got it all on film. Picture that found the papers all over the place was the one with the gorilla on the gator's back, bouncing. The powder flying out Lazarus' nose and mouth made it look real spooky, like he was giving up the ghost. Front pages had big headlines about a gorilla raising a gator from the dead at the Alligator Zoo-Park. Mr. Cotter made them include a map. Heard some ghost hunters visited soon after.

The picture Jeffers kept framed was Lazarus all propped up on his elbows looking proud as he could be, fresh back from being dead.

23

Jeffers'd been putting it out there as an escape act. Man gets rolled up in a minivan with a brick on the gas pedal, chained up and such and somebody would strap some dynamite to the thing and hope he'd book it on out of there with some kinda quickness. But I think people were coming more for the chicken. I saved the coupon, stuck it in my pocket.

The ad in the Money Pages said something like, "Free! Twenty Pieces of Wings for Jeffers in One Pieces." Señor Luis put that ad in there. Wrote it his ownself. He was looking for a bump, like he wasn't plenty busy. But he paid for the van rental and the nineteen-dollar insurance. He was going to give away a whole bundle of chicken. Señor Luis said if Jeffers pulled off his next magnificent trick, he'd offer a free twenty-piece chicken wings to everybody that was there. Don't know how he'd have known that people were there, but they sure-enough showed up. I know he meant to put a little star next to the offer saying folks had to buy something to get something, but the Money Pages forgot, or he forgot somehow or another and that little note didn't make it in the ad. Instead, Jeffers drew a crowd and they wanted them some of that chicken.

Jeffers set the show up for daytime down at the racetrack so everybody could see. There was a whole mess a people when I drove up in the NAILR. Jeffers was right behind me in the rental van.

The racetrack sat up on a little hill looking off to one side over the river, the other three had some woods all around. Fire department was there. They would push the van in the river if things got to blowing up on him.

Folks weren't there for the magic. They'd heard stories about Bobby the raccoon and his fixed toes. More than likely, they saw Jeffers in the papers, dressed up like a gorilla, riding old Lazarus back to life. Mr. Cotter sure had. He had a host of mermaids out there selling tee-shirts. The papers had stories all over the place. Folks were feeling like Jeffers was likely to fix them, too, and get them some chicken at the same time.

I swear people were rolling friends and family up in wheelchairs that hadn't seen the light of day in sometime. Some of these people were looking like perhaps they'd been dug up by some hungry relative. It was family night at the racetrack. I'd hand it to Jeffers. Man wasn't nervous. Not one bit. He took one look around that big congregation and nodded like it was just about time for them to show up like that.

Señor Luis was there letting folks know the coupon was only good after the show. I was surprised because it wasn't often that I saw him not drinking a Bud Light at his bar and yelling at people. But he was ready for a time. He had him the Casa de Chiné party truck rolled up there near the race track and some people dishing up wings on the spot. I was hungry and we went straight over there and got us some hot-hot. Things weren't going all that great for Señor Luis. They were already running out of the little dreamy wings. I ordered ten and counted nine on my paper plate.

"Jimmy, I'm just thinking you already ate one."

"I'm not imagining this. Don't even have any chicken in my teeth, no sauce on my mouth." I bared my teeth and showed them through the little window.

The crowd was still coming in slow, but sure. Then I saw the buses. Yellow school buses all filled up with folks rolling in on the dirt road, kids starting to file off. Whole bunch of little kids all started tripping over themselves and hustling over to the taco trucks. Teacher walked up to Señor Luis.

"We had to skip the MacDonalds. They're remodeling the play place." Three more yellow buses of kids were rolling up, squeaking brakes and all. Diesel smoke pouting out of the tailpipes, settling down on the ground like a heavy comforter.

Señor Luis looked like he was going to run away. The line of kids was stretching out down the track and they were about as whiny as could be. My boys might've been in there someplace so I kinda started hiding off to the side of the truck.

I heard some scrambling and such coming from the truck and took a look. Señor Luis was letting them have it.

"Whatchu mean we're out of wings?"

"No más después de esto." The man in the apron covered in orange colored sauce shrugged him off and pointed to a carton of frozen wings.

"Esta no posiblemente!" Señor Luis got himself a little more riled up and the man dressed-up in the wing sauce did about the same.

"Pequeños búfalos volaron!" The man hooked his hands together like he was making a shadow puppet, flapping away like a butterfly.

I could read sign language.

Jeffers was hearing it too. Big event like that with no food wasn't going to be a good look. There was a whole bunch of hungry folks out there and Jeffers couldn't really afford to be dealing with another angry crowd. Wasn't much of an escape route for me to scoop him up and take off through, anyhow.

The line kept growing. People were taking their lunch breaks and unemployment breaks away from drinking big bottles of Carlo Rossi and crunching empty cans to come out there and have them a show. Saw Miriam driving up and Jeffers left to go chat with her. Meantime, I kept on listening to Señor Luis get heated.

"Dos casos? Tenemos *dos* casos?" He was slinging boxes around that little camper-looking trailer. Hustling his folks outta the way and generally just being mean while they were still tossing wings and putting them on plates, shorting every one of them by a wing or two. I saw Jeffers over there with Miriam. They were doing some whisper-fighting, maybe some necking, but probably not. Couldn't hear a word. Miriam saw me and stopped.

"Jimmy." She nodded. Jeffers turned around.

Miriam got out of the NAILR, but left it running. She got in the rental and I was feeling puzzled. Jeffers followed her, but she wasn't having it.

It wasn't long before she drove off the way she came. I thought Jeffers must've been getting her out of there before the crowd got too testy. It wasn't hard to see it coming.

Señor Luis walked out of the trailer and over to the waiting line. "Perdóname! Escuse-me, folks." Kids were slapping each other and people were jabbering. They were hungry for sure. "'Scuse-me!" Señor Luis tried again. "We are low on the wings." People got real quiet. "We have some for you. You have to share. There is not enough for all of you in the line." There was lots of grumbling coming from those folks. Not sure if it was their bellies or their mouths. The line wasn't breaking up. The crowd wasn't giving up their hope. "This is what we have left." Señor Luis held up a paper basket of wings. He was holding out a little for his own belly.

Folks were all focused on Señor Luis and his basket. The line was breaking up and they were scattering about all pissed and hungry. Jeffers walked over next to Señor Luis and talked to them.

"We'll bring out what we've got for you. Find a spot where y'all can get settled for the show."

Folks listened to Jeffers. They moseyed on and milled elsewhere. Me and Jeffers walked back over to the rental. There was a little baby alligator in the back. That was the first time I saw Chubby. I was about to ask Jeffers where the rental went when I saw Miriam come rolling back up.

"What's going on?"

"Jimmy, we've got to get on with the trick. You ready?"

"I'm ready."

Me and Jeffers got to moving pretty quick. Folks were settling in their lawn chairs on the old tarmac. They were all looking hungry, like they might go on and eat me and Jeffers if the trick wasn't up to snuff. We needed to get them out of there and off to lunch before they got testy.

The crowd was grumbling and lined up ready for a trick. The healing could wait for the next go 'round if there was one. Jeffers pulled the rental van to the starting line and I was right there with him. I opened the back gate and he handed me the hand-

185

cuffs and I went on and put them on him. He held his hands up to the crowd and I side-eyed a few dozen cases of wings there in the back of the van. Thought kind of crossed my mind that maybe he'd been holding out.

"No way out, folks!" He yanked his hands apart real hard to show he couldn't shake off the cuffs. I got the rope out of the back of the rental. He held one end, cuffs and all. I held the other and we stretched out the whole thing so folks could see. Then I started wrapping him up in that rope. Tied it off real tight right there in front of everybody. I wondered how he was going to get out myself. There was a whole shit ton of dynamite in the back of that van. More than I wanted to mess with, but Jeffers had me set the timer and press "START." Miriam had been driving a bomb around town. Wonder if she even knew.

"Three minutes y'all! That's what I got!" Those people started hustling up fast as they could and scraping those lawn chairs and camping chairs back a little. They just scoot-scooted like they didn't think Jeffers was going to move that van. Couldn't really blame them. They held their hands over their eyes—waiting on a shuttle to lift off.

"Alright. Jimmy, here, is going to get this van moving!" He was moving a little quicker than usual. Think the mix-up at the last show had him a little spooked. His cool self had melted off in front of those hungry people. I was just hoping he didn't get reckless.

Jeffers was all wrapped up and sat down on the bumper of that rental. I grabbed him by the legs and pushed him up in the back of the van, closed the trunk lid just barely. There wasn't much room left. Slapped the back of the van for effect. I'd seen that in some movies or something. Then I walked around to the front and grabbed the brick off the driver's side floor. I held it up to the crowd. Some of them cheered, some held their breath. I was holding mine. The van was on, so I revved it a little in neutral. More cheers started coming from those folks. I put the brick on the gas and it dropped to the floor. I checked the shoelace holding the steering wheel straight. That van sounded pissed and whiny getting its RPM's on up to the top like that. Then I yanked it down in drive and jumped out of the way. It spun its tires a second, then got to rolling down the track. The timer was on three minutes, probably about two left, but there was only about thirty seconds worth of track at the most.

I stood next to Miriam. We watched. The track was running out fast.

"What's with the baby gator?"

"Chubby." We stared and watched the van. It was moving quick.

"What's with Chubby?"

"That's about all Jeffers says I'm ready to care for."

"Y'all trying?"

Some of the kids behind us started crying. Then, slow but sure enough, the van made a turn. It turned just enough in a big circle to get to coming back around back around the way it came. I thought I had the steering wheel tied off right. It was just a shoestring. Lots of folks started crying, then. Some were jumping up out of their chairs, teachers were leaving their kids.

"Been there. Had to quit it. I thought I was ready. 'Parently, I wasn't."

"When was that?"

"Recent. Jeffers thinks Chubby's enough for me to take care of."

That rental van was coming back straight for the crowd.

"You got the windows rolled down?"

"I do." She looked over at me, chin quivering a little. "Thanks for asking."

"My ba..." couldn't quite get the word out. The van braked hard, smoke coming off the tires and burning up some new bald spots. No way those wheels would roll right again.

Through the window I saw Jeffers there in the driver seat, hands at ten and two.

He parked that van about a hundred yards down the track and got to running back our way with a big grin on his face. He had escaped and couldn't have been happier when he got to what was left of the crowd. Me and Miriam hadn't moved.

A few folks were clapping and wiping away tears on their t-shirts and making up with the people they had got up and left. About that time that van blew up right off its wheels. I could feel the heat on my face like a campfire and a wave, bobbing in the river when a boat went by. That whole carcass of a van was in the air for a second. Never seen anything like it. Looked like a shower of fire-works blowing off in just about every which way. Then the little flames floated down from the sky, landing with miniature thuds all around.

It was raining chicken wings. The little charred chicken-bits floated down slow like they had smoke parachutes.

Didn't take long for people to figure out Jeffers was feeding their very souls. Kids started wrastling with each other, grownups were grabbing wings out of the sky, burning their fingertips and licking them after they finished each wing. It got kind of wicked, but everybody got a bite. Rumblings started about Jeffers and the magic wings. Jeffers had somehow taken a basket of wings and turned it into a snack for every man, woman, and child out there. Even saw a dog or two hacking on the bones. We brushed a little dirt off, sure, and there wasn't any sauce, but it was filling, and got a whole bunch a folks convinced of something otherworldly.

24

M e and Jeffers were out of Hot Pockets. There was this squirrel outside that kept going up and down the tree, building a nest and chattering at pinecones. We'd spent nearly all of Jeffers' last check on a whole bundle of mushrooms that let us see the squirrel's thoughts in color. After two days of hurling our questions at the squirrel and listening, really listening, for an answer in purple or blue, we remembered we needed to eat. Aunt Becky hadn't been home in at least as long, and we thought for a minute she might be in that nest up there just watching us the whole time, maybe judging, maybe not and moving real spastic here and there. Then we thought she might give us a little cash to buy some Hot Pockets, so we tried to climb up there. It wasn't her, and we needed some food on the cheap.

My van was stripped of everything but wheels and the sexiness that comes with a super-fast machine. We had the radio dialed in on some mariachi.

"Keep winding." Jeffers was turning the knob. Streams of lines, motion, were flowing out of his hand in circles. Little blue and gold sparkles popped with every rotation. Fireworks of some other world of motion and magic, spirits working on his side. Sitting shotgun, it was his job to wind the radio and hold it right so it picked up signal and we could hear. He tried to turn up the volume but it was already higher than the knob should twist.

"I'm winding. You just watch the road." This is how our talking was going. Something big was sitting between us, but it wasn't Denny. She was gone and took the windshield wipers. It was something heavy, a conversation we couldn't spit out. When we tried, the center console swallowed up the words.

The morning was best for driving—while the fog was still thick on the road and we could plow through a fog bank with it sucking and swirling behind us. We kept the mariachi pumping.

A squirrel and something looking like a big lizard scooted across the road in a real hurry, one chasing the other and I near permanently arted—what we called the flat colors that were left in the tracks of the animal's afterlife—the both of them on the cement when Jeffers yanked the wheel out of my hand.

Jeffers swung the wheel and I swear we could've been spinning on the icy rings of Saturn. We hopped the curb and I was stomping the floorboards for about a minute when we finally swiped a row of bushes, just real gentle like they were giving the van a belly scratch and making the back wheels spin, then came to a stop. The radio hit the windshield and I hit the steering wheel.

I pushed off the dash and back into my seat. The radio was sitting up on the dash blaring some fuzz and cracked in a couple-three pieces. We sat there in the fuzz and the bushes for a minute until it started dying again. I just stared at the pieces and started to get a little choked up. We'd been working that thing and hearing it talk at us for years. I should've known then that things were setting up to come to an end. That radio was trying to tell me just that, but when the world's all funky it's real hard to listen to the simple stuff. Jeffers was hazy and not moving much. Just looking out the window and being real still.

"It's broke." I thought I might have to wind him up to get him moving again. Jeffers was still just sitting, staring out on the world through that wavy windshield, cooked from years of no cooling off. Jeffers had eyes like two marbled blue bowling balls all waxed up and polished, rolling and slipping down the lane. Real heavy when they hit. I came to see that stare as him being somewhere else entirely. He wasn't there just then. He was hearing the birds in the trees and listening to the wind change directions when it hit branches and leaves. He must've known the songs in the hot breeze as familiar as some kids' nursery rhyme. I came to believe it later.

"Why'd you do a thing like that?"

"It's not right."

"What's not right? You yanking us off the road?"

"It ain't good, Jimmy." He was rubbing his head and his eyes with his palms all open looking like he might be about to cry or something. "Can't be offing them critters."

"You've lost it, for sure."

"Those creatures were just trying to get breakfast. Don't care about another living thing but yourself."

"We can eat them if you're wanting to. I've got no problem with that."

"I don't want to eat them. Just shouldn't be messing with them like that."

"Who's messing? They're still chasing each other back there. We missed." I did see in the mirror that I might've tagged the lizard.

"I feel it every time we hit them."

"I do too, dammit. The van bumps a little. But that doesn't suck all the enjoyment out of the drive for me like you are right now."

"There's no enjoyment in killing critters. I mean I feel it. Like when we been eating the caps for a day or two solid and all the sudden we got the trees talking our language. You know?"

"No idea. Trees don't ever talk to me. Had a couple dogs tell me about their days, but that was on some of that stuff Hecho gave me."

I pulled the rigged coat hanger and popped my door. I couldn't open it because of the bush, so I walked through the back of the van and out the hatch. Looked around to make sure all the wheels were still there. I thought about the possibility of the cops cruising over and finding us, pupils big and dark as the eclipse, parked in a bush, so I climbed back through the hatch and pulled the rope on the door to close it.

"Let's get a move on before the cops get here," I said.

Jeffers shimmied a little at the thought. I dropped the Windstar into drive and we started wiggling out of the bush and on down the sidewalk till the tires found the road again. We'd found the wilderness. I was looking for mercy.

"We're going to have to take your van till the radio gets fixed. We can't cruise around with no radio." The radio worked in the NAILR, but the noise came out of one speaker—the back left one.

"Jimmy. I believe I'm hungry. You hungry?"

I was.

There was something downright beautiful about a cup of coffee tasting like a cigarette, so we went to the Waffle House and put music on the jukebox to gyrate our brains till the caffeine kicked in. The booth-back bent and bounced me forward when I sat down, and the plastic menu stuck to the table from somebody else's orange juice or something.

"Always is a little funny when I can't get the mat to come off the table."

"What're you thinking it is?"

"Who knows? Syrup?"

"Could be. But why's the mat on top of the syrup? You'd think the syrup would go on top."

Teri walked up to take our order, or at least get a drop on what'd been going on. Teri, along with every other waitress, made sure to take good care of Jeffers. He was a real big deal. He may not have paid for a meal for weeks at a time.

"Hey," Teri said. She set a water glass down in front of Jeffers. "Y'all're early."

"Don't I know." I said that. But she didn't pay me no mind. She was trying real hard to get to meat gazing and was already chewing on some gum at six-thirty in the morning. Probably working on last night's gin and the same piece of Nicorette to go with it.

Jeffers ordered our usual for us: coffee, patty melts with packs of mayo and hashbrowns smothered, covered, and chunked. Ordered me a water, too. Teri made a big deal out of knocking a fork on the floor and was able to pick it up on her third try bending down. Could've knocked her over with an elbow to the seat, but Jeffers was in a mood.

"You know, Señor Luis has been telling me that he'll toss a little coin my way if I can bring him some interesting meat."

"Jimmy, you still aren't digging what I'm burying." Teri brought the coffee. Tried to make dropping creamer packets on the table look more than serviceable. "Besides, Señor Luis makes wings. How're you going to fry up a squirrel and a lizard to make wings like he's doing?"

"Be right back with your food," Teri said, like I didn't even exist. She picked up our straw paper.

Jeffers had a point. I peeled back a couple creamer tops and dropped them in my coffee. Opened a third one and drank it. Jeffers was spinning his cup, probably thinking about magic and lizards. I looked out the glass front of the diner. The House of China sign was glowing on top of the Windstar, draining my battery, and the fog was still thick. It made the sign look real official and powerful. My battery would be alright.

"Why're you giving me such a hard time?"

I thought back to all the squirrels, I could still see their faces in different states of surprise when they found the front end of the NAILR, me riding shotgun and cranking the radio while we howled.

"Was it 'cause I was driving today?"

Jeffers just shook his head and drank some coffee. He didn't bother with the cream. I don't think I would've either, but I didn't trust their milk to drink. I liked having some milk in the morning.

"It's about respecting something."

"I should be talking to you about respect." I drank a creamer.

"What?"

"Got her a gator instead of a baby. Didn't even tell me."

"You need to know everything, Jimmy? It's your choice to wander around in the dark. Can't see a thing in front of you. But don't be talking about Chubby."

Teri dropped the hot plates on the table. I thought I saw her try to tuck a napkin in Jeffers' shirt. Could've been my imagination.

"Anything else I can do?" Teri looked starved and made up at the same time. Those ladies were always looking for Jeffers to sweep them up. Jeffers shook his head and she must've pulled a couple muscles trying to keep that smile on her face when she turned.

"I guess I'm not getting you."

"I guess not."

I doctored my sandwich and got my napkins ready, squeezed ketchup on my hash browns, then his. We were real quiet and worked on eating.

"Jimmy, only thing I was left with from my folks was a picture of a barn and a man-sized teddy bear. I've been thinking a lot about that lately."

Pops left me with his rubber band gun. That was about it. He used it to keep the cat in check. I used it on my boys, sometimes my momma.

"I know about your bear."

If it was a competition to have as little as possible it'd be a push. Jeffers was really pushing the whole "What are we doing, anyway?" thing lately. It wasn't a lot of fun having to always think about the point of stuff. That was all me and Jeffers said during the meal. We listened to the jukebox play droning old men talking about missed loves, special ladies and hurt feelings. It made me start to miss my friend.

I paid for my meal. Jeffers' was on the house.

"Thanks, Teri," I said when we were leaving. She didn't know I was there. One of the cooks waved to me. "It was good," I called. He nodded. Outside, we climbed back into the van. Jeffers tried to wind the radio to fill up the whole bunch of empty we were sitting in. I drove. People were getting out on the roads. I hit it hard and let that good potato cannon muffler cough, letting loose some hot breath. I passed some folks riding their bicycles down the middle of the road like a neon streak of stupid. Normally, I'd get giddy to throw my empties at their helmets, but this morning I just had a sick belly. I wasn't real sure if it was the creamer curdling or the company.

Well, I was uncomfortable. Not super uncomfortable real sick-like, but kinda uncomfortable. Like when I would be sitting there flushing and the water would splash back up. Just like things weren't going quite right like they was supposed to. Right about then, I remembered the beer in the small cooler behind my seat. I had one left and I for sure wasn't going to be offering one up to Jeffers. It'd at least cool things down in my belly. I turned left back toward the river and started reaching down and behind me to snag that last beer, but the little igloo top was stuck on that cooler and was trying to give me extra heartburn. Like I didn't already get me enough from the patty melt.

"Jimmy!" Jeffers yelled. First thing Jeffers said to me in plenty of minutes and sure enough it came along with a *THUMP*.

I hit the brakes and we stopped pretty quick. My poor Windstar was hissing and I still wasn't sure what we hit 'cause I hadn't been looking in the first place. I'd finally gotten that top off the cooler and somehow didn't drop the beer, so I cracked the top and took a sip. Looked over at Jeffers.

"Man?"

"Deer."

First deer I ever thumped. It sure did a number on the Windstar.

"Did it on purpose?" Jeffers was steaming.

"Now why'd I go on and beat up my van just to piss you off? Wouldn't that be some stupid shit."

Jeffers swung his door open and scooted out. I took a second to myself with my beer and got to thinking about having to ride my bike everywhere. How my legs would be so tired and how hard it was to carry a twelve pack, much less twenty-four on the handlebars 'cause they just weren't made right to hold it.

"Jimmy! Gimme that beer."

I slid out of my door and started making my way 'round to the front, not wanting to look but kinda having to look at the damage to my van. It was beat up pretty bad. Good-sized deer made his mark, busted my radiator for sure. Van was leaking, deer wasn't leaking all that bad.

"Jimmy, gimme the beer." Jeffers was cradling that deer head in his lap, it was honking a little, breathing all heavy and such. I figured Jeffers for needing a drink after all this. It was my last beer, but I handed it to him anyway, thought of it as a peace offering. No sooner did I hand it over when Jeffers started letting the deer suck his lips up on my can.

"Man, what the hell are you doing?" First the deer wrecked my van then he got after my beer. I for sure didn't want to be drinking after him. Jeffers just held a finger up to his lips and kept letting that deer suck down my beer. I swear I heard that thing start guzzling. I saw it in his eyes, deer was perking up, looking straight at me. I didn't like it, so I went and got back in the van so I could think. Had my chin on the steering wheel when I saw that booger get up. That deer just stood on up limber as could be. He looked straight at me and snorted, kinda sneezed at me. Then he walked around my side of the van, looking like he was circling, staring me down.

"Sorry," I said. That deer moseyed on down the road. "You took my beer!" I yelled at him. Jeffers was getting back in the van. "You going to fix my van, too?"

"That's your problem." Jeffers tossed the empty in the back and it rattled around, sounding all empty and mean.

"That was my last beer." A dozen or so—maybe less—thoughts rambled through my head. "How do you suppose we get home?"

"We're probably going to have to walk. Better get used to it." I thought I heard a deer laughing at me so I turned around. But it wasn't. I should've hitched a harness up to that bastard and let him pull me home.

"We've got a ways to walk." I unplugged my House of China sign, got out and stood on the side of the sill while I yanked the topper off my car. Kids loved stealing those signs, and Señor Luis would make me pay for it, for sure. Then we got to walking. It was quiet for plenty a ways down the road. We walked the river and watched the fog break. The sun got to being all orange and red peeking over the edge of trees on the other bank. I wondered what they saw over this way. Sunsets, I guessed.

"I've got Judd helping me." He was watching the ground.

"With the next trick."

"Just like that?" I stopped, put the topper down on dirt, ready to get into it. He kept walking. "We could've ate that deer!"

"Wasn't dead yet." He was still looking forward.

"Seemed pretty close!"

"Yep."

"Jeffers, when I'm dying, you going to fix me with a beer?"

He paused a second, but didn't turn around.

"Nope. Won't be here."

25

Something was dead up under the house. Momma had stopped by looking for a fifth of vodka. Found the bottle she stuck in the cushion and tossed it in an Igloo cooler, kicked me and the boys out of the house until things smelled right again. It didn't smell much better outside. I'd walked by Pete's and he told me something similar was going on around his place. It was seeming like the whole park was smelling.

I could stick a shrimp on the porch to steam it. It was warm outside and things had started getting wily. My real needs were a chair and a roof with at least a little A/C, so I started trying to solve problems. I found myself wallowing around under the house, elbows poked out to the sides, sliding on my belly, pondering about things. There was two feet of crawlspace under the house, just about enough for me to go sniffing for dead meat. I bobbed my head up every now and then to flare my nostrils, then got back to wiggling around to another hot, wet corner. Never did find the smell, but I did lay there behind the wooden steps looking when Miriam walked up to the house.

I was lost to her in the shadows. She was in a hurry, moving around like a moth, kinda light, but also a little lost-looking and spastic. I watched her hesitate for a minute. She'd start walking to the house, then turn around, hand on her chin. A snake slithered up next to my foot and I kicked it in the head.

"Shoo," I was whispering.

It slid over the dirt, kept its belly cool and moved on. I dug my nails in the dirt and got to watching some more.

I almost popped my head out through the steps but didn't want to talk. The smell was pretty strong and I was having to breathe through my mouth, teeth hanging out, getting dry. Finally, Miriam walked up the steps, knocking dust in my eyes through the cracks. She didn't wear shoes. Never did. A little bit of light found its way through the floor above, and I could see she was still turning back and forth, trying to do something and trying to not. Fast as she came, she left, floating down the stairs and down the road. Folks were losing their minds in the heat. Maybe she needed something, I don't know. She'd said Jeffers was leaving her out too. Really bothered her. He said it was for her own good. We'd been there to help him as long as he'd let us in, making posters, doing what we could, anything we could. Don't know how it was that a man could cut out his best friend and his girl, but maybe he didn't know how to trust. I'd been nothing but loyal. Miriam was as loyal as she knew how to be.

I kept sniffing and looking. The ground was a cool place to be. I rolled around in the piles of round-glass vodka bottles till I found a broken one and settled myself down. I smiled, knowing Momma and Denny'd been stashing them under there for years. Not for any real reason but knowing that the garbage truck rarely made it back in the park. Near every time it did, a tow truck had to come with it. I thought for a second there were some pretty flowers growing up under there too. Got to wondering how something so nice could grow in the dark. But I was wrong. It was the fine bunch of silk flowers I'd picked up for Denny back when I tried to perk her up with something other than a king size pack of Reese's. She broke the vase and started playing "Free Bird" on blast a couple years later. That was before she wore a path trying to return her ring to the Kmart every couple months.

I kept scooting.

The shiver hit from my head, making my blood all cold clear down to my tail. A breeze would have to be about zero degrees to make me feel like that. I let my eyes focus on the little numbers that for sure could add up to a million. Red and black, hearts and spades.

Pick a card.

The pile of cards, I slipped through the tiniest cut in the linoleum floor, one at a time. I would sit Indian-style across from my best friend. He was desperate trying to figure out the only trick I ever kept from him. Had me do the same trick over and over.

Where did it go?

Where did it go?

A thousand times over.

I broke the rule. Same audience, same trick, but he never figured it out. There was a whole universe of magical frustration piled up under the house, nearly touching the floor above. The cards were a single mass, thin pieces of coated paper that turned into a hidden mountain. With time and heat and water, clubs became diamonds. The trucks and the bulldozers would come. When they came for the trailer, they'd have to get through the mountain. There was nowhere else for my magic. My only big trick was stuck in a single spot in the floor of my trailer, a spot I found running from a backhand, tripping and pulling up the edge of a shitty laid down floor. It was the last edge I would ever step off. I thought I'd found something special, something that was unknown and mysterious. But that was kid stuff. Jeffers had taken the disappointment of not knowing and pushed off the floor and into the world. I was still stuck to that linoleum. The alligators in the park thought they had a shot at Jeffers every time he stepped in the pit to do a trick. They stashed bones and I stashed cards. My magic couldn't move. I played my only angle till it was nothing but a pile of wet shit. Jeffers was the only one that was free.

I pulled myself out into the sunlight and let my skin warm up from the cold of realization. I sat down and held onto my knees for a minute. I needed to eat, but my van was a wreck. After we hit the deer, I'd left it in the street till I could get it towed. I was pretty sure it didn't need much to get running, but I didn't have it in me to work on it. By the time it was dropped in my front yard there was a village of dirt daubers and bees living in there, buzzing and pollinating. My bike was stashed around the side. The tires were near flat and let me feel every bump on the road as I got headed to the MacDonalds. It felt alright to get some air moving around me and made it a little less difficult to get a breath without smelling something awful. I didn't get far before I heard an engine behind me, felt a machine creeping up on my back wheel. When I turned around I saw Jeffers. I pulled off and he stopped next to me.

"Where you going?" He looked normal as could be. Things must not have been bothering him. Definitely hadn't been having a day like mine, or he was pretty good at hiding it. "Hungry?"

"That's where I was headed." He was waving his hand, telling me to come on.

"Get in. Let's get some food."

I stashed my bike in the bushes by the road. Probably where I found it in the first place. Then I got in.

"Man, you smell awful. What've you been doing?" His nose was all scrunched up like a pig. We started driving.

"Been up under my house."

"Why?"

"Tryin' to figure out what's smelling so bad. The whole park is stinking." Jeffers pulled the collar of his shirt up, sniffed himself.

"You check yourself?" I didn't bother. We rode in some quiet for a minute.

"Miriam's mad with me." The sun reflected off the windshield, hitting his sunglasses hard. He'd started wearing some fancy blacked out numbers that made him look big time.

"Why's that?" Didn't feel like the right time to tell him she'd come around.

"Same as you."

"You ready for your trick?" Took everything I had to ask about it. I couldn't look at him while I did. I looked at billboards for attorneys and the big orange construction signs on the side of the road. They needed more lanes and more cars and people.

"About as ready as I'll ever be, I guess." He took a deep breath. "You gonna come out and see it?"

"I guess."

"Jimmy. Something happens to me. I'll be back."

"What's the trick?"

"Can't tell you. But you mark it down. I'll be back. Three days."

"What's got you worrying?" I couldn't see it, sunglasses or not.

We pulled into the MacDonalds, found a pretty prime spot. Jeffers put the NAILR in park and paused for a second.

"It's a big one." I saw the sweat on his nose, little beads welling up, and I knew he was having some nerves. He had on a good front, good looks, smile trying to hold on, cool and calm, but he was burning up on his insides. Fire catching layer by layer, making its way up like smoke in a chimney till it reached the top.

"Sorry I couldn't help." I got out and hit the door of the car next to us. Got a little concerned till I realized it was Pete's. I guess Jeffers had told Pete and Andy we were headed over there 'cause they were waiting inside. They had a nice table with a bunch of seats but no food. I didn't realize it was supposed to be Jeffers' treat.

Jeffers didn't ask what we wanted. I sat down in a middle seat at the table.

"What's wrong with you, Jimmy?" Andy was asking. He looked concerned, for real. I must've been wearing a look on my face. Pete went over to help Jeffers carry the food. He was never much for being worried about feelings. I think his only feelings must've been in his belly.

"I'm alright. Just hungry." I was feeling it. Jeffers'd been messing around with my life a little much over the last few days, but I couldn't get the worries to shake. It bothered me a whole bunch that Miriam was feeling it, too.

Pete and Jeffers walked up. Pete held up the tray of food like he'd been the one buying. Tommy walked in the door and came up to the table, sat down on an end. Jeffers put the tray down and sat down to my left. He had everybody around him he wanted when Judd walked in.

"Sorry I'm late." Came up and gave Jeffers a hug.

"What're you wanting, Judd?" Pete was asking. Judd looked kinda lost.

"I invited him." Jeffers got to trying to settle Pete. "He's helping me out with the trick tomorrow."

"You don't have enough help?" Pete was looking over at me, and I appreciated him about as much as I ever had.

"Can I get one?" Judd took a box of fries off the tray. Jeffers passed out the rest of the fries, one box at a time to everybody around the table, to a chorus of grumbled *thanks*. The Filet o'fishies came next. Pete handed out cups of coke. Jeffers held his up.

"To the big trick," he said. Sweat still showing up on his nose, smile hanging on his face like some beat down moon.

Cheers.

Cheers.

Cheers.

Was coming from everybody. I concerned myself with peeling the Monopoly scratch-off from the back of my fries. Got another Baltic.

PART 3

The Gospel of Jimmy

26

The party started again when I rubbed my eyes and smelled last night's fried shrimp on my hands. We blew the best meal on the first night. I pulled on the neck of my shirt and let the breeze cool off my heart. It was throbbing like a two-stroke outboard and I was pretty sure I still hadn't sweated out all the booze and bud from the night before. That was a relief, 'cause it meant I could get super-hammered again with less expense.

I wanted breakfast and a glass of juice. Something simple, just to make me feel human again for a minute. Miriam's house was stacked and littered with bodies and I was pretty sure her A/C was out. It definitely wasn't running. I shuffled over a couple folks, kicking them along the way to make sure they weren't dead. That's why we were all there, anyway. Waiting on a dead man.

Miriam's thermostat was on the wall, hanging on fresh yellow paint and high class. She'd graduated from the window unit by getting a job at the fro-yo shop and cashing disability checks. I fixed A/C's for a living and still had a window unit. I checked her thermostat and it claimed to be running, but I knew it was lying. There was a constant drip running down my legs and I knew for sure it was sweat. When I turned around, Miriam was standing there.

"Did he show?" She looked hopeful and disappointed all at the same time.

"Haven't tripped over him yet. But I don't see him lying around here in one of these heaps of sweat."

"I'm sorry, I know my unit's been out."

"You know I'd be more than happy to fix it. Just got to ask."

"I know. Been busy." She had a purple mustache and a bottle of Carlo Rossi hanging down from her arm by a finger. "You still think he's coming."

I held my hand out and she passed me the jug. It wasn't exactly breakfast juice, but it tasted grapey enough and was purple, so I sucked on it for a second or two and took another look around. I watched the thermostat on the wall, swore I could see it crawling up.

"He told me he'd be here." I took a second pull on the Carlo, real greedy, then passed it back to her.

"You got a purple mustache." She smiled. I didn't tell her that she did too. It was the first time I'd seen her smile in a couple days— definitely the first time since the trick. She'd been real worried about Jeffers before that.

"I'm goin' to check the unit." Seemed like as good a time to do it.

She hiccupped and kind of swallowed it, tucked her chin up to her chest and made her eyes all big. I thought she looked like a fish of some kind, but better. "Thanks, Jimmy. For everything." Then she started tearing up again, for like the four hundredth time in the past couple days, and I turned my head. I walked off to the door and pulled it open. Shit was bright, minivans were damn-near rubbing up on each other all over the lawn. I checked a couple and they weren't actually touching, just looking like it. We didn't need any more mini-vans birthing babies on the lawn. I snorted a little at the thought. The weeds felt up my shirt and tickled my belly, and I felt a little better that Miriam could afford a thermostat but still didn't cut her lawn. I grabbed up a stick and hacked at the weeds, hoping I could get a look at any slicked-up snake before he caught me.

I couldn't even see the A/C unit, the weeds had all but eaten it up. Don't know when the last time the thing worked, but it couldn't have been anytime recent. A vine wrapped down in there, all around the fan blade. I tore it off, careful for my fingers 'cause I'd seen some get lost with a chomp in these things before. It still didn't start and I was melting. I snorted hard and hocked everything I could muster from the back of my throat. Then I fired that business down into the fan's main bearing. Nothing.

I kicked the shit out of that thing then. Kicked it with every bit of frustration and embarrassment I had been left with. Still nothing. Sweat dropped from the tip of my nose. A mosquito landed next to the salty pool on the A/C cover. I watched it take a look, maybe at itself. My hand must've been a mighty big surprise. The machine shook with the thud. It sputtered and woke, grunted like some big-ass ancient beast—like Lazarus—and I thought about Jeffers.

I needed another drink and found a beer can on one of the railroad ties in the backyard. I got real hopeful and picked the can from its seat. When I shook it, a bee came buzzing out looking a little tipsy. I saved the bee and polished off the last quarter beer.

I pulled the sliding glass door. Locked. With all those fools stacked inside, Miriam still had the door locked. I rapped on the glass and Chubby came tapping along. He rubbed his teeth on the glass then slid his neck up against it. Even the three-foot baby gator was looking to cool himself off a little. Pete stumbled up. He shooed Chubby away from the door with his foot, popped the latch and opened it just wide enough for me to squeeze through.

Pete lit a smoke and washed it down with a pull off Miriam's Carlo from the counter. A bag of Doritos was open, mouth wide, next to it.

"Shit. I sure wish I could turn this place right-side up." Pete's dark eyes looked even darker with the circles around them. "That breakfast?" He snagged an orange chip from the bag and licked his fingers after sticking the whole thing in his mouth. Miriam sat down and brought the bottle with her.

"Ugh. He show up?" Pete prodded at me. He rubbed his temples with his fingers and stared at the counter.

I shook my head.

"Not yet." Miriam chimed. The Carlo was back in her head helping her believe. I reached for the bottle.

"At least something did." He pointed up at the ceiling vent. "What else you got?" Pete was still rubbing his temples. The Dorito wasn't quite doing it for him. Miriam opened the freezer and a cloud of cold came fogging out. The air in the room was still steamy despite the A/C's struggles to keep up.

"We got a pork chop loin." Miriam stared into the cold, mouth half open. "Um." She pursed her lips and blew cold in a smoke ring while she swung the door back-and-forth. "That's about it." She pulled the pork out of the freezer and dropped it on the counter like a paperweight. "We've got to let it thaw a little. Otherwise it'll turn out tough." She put a beer on the table in front of me.

An old deck of Sun Cruz Casino playing cards was spread out in a red half-circle on the table. It looked at me like some big old toothy smile. If Jeffers was there he would've shown us something new.

"Want to see a trick?"

Nobody said a thing.

Pete slunk over to the table and into a chair.

"What the hell?" Pete yelped and jumped back up. Chubby tapped across the linoleum and out from under the table. "That little booger nipped my heel!"

My foot was asleep, but I was thankful that Pete got the nipping. It never really hurt, yet. But it was unsettling, like a nasty little promise of things to come. Miriam laughed and hiccupped and apologized while Andy found his way from the floor to the kitchen sink. He spit up everything he didn't want to ever see again.

"Hey, wash that down, okay?" Miriam was too sweet. "Spray some of that soap in there too. Pete, your brother can't hold liquor worth a shit." Andy hunched over the sink, holding his weight on his elbows. His feet were barely on the floor. Pete walked over to the counter, grabbing the frozen pork stick, then over to his brother. He held the pork on the back of Andy's neck, then pulled the waist of his brother's jeans out and dropped the frozen meat down the back of his pants.

"Muthaflughhhhhhhh..."

Andy gagged and gurgled, wagging his pork tail in the back of his drawers while he opened up some more free space in his stomach. He turned on the faucet and the disposal while he stuck his whole head under the nozzle. When his head popped up he looked pretty rough. He yanked the pork out of his pants and flung the whole damn chop toward us like a meat boomerang. My reaction time was a smidge off, and I would still swear the meat grazed me before it went cracking through the glass door and into the backyard. Chubby was making a break for it while the glass was still falling from the frame. That sonofabitch was either jailbreaking or chasing that frozen meat club.

"Get Chubby!" Miriam yelled. Pete yanked me out of the chair and we stumbled out in the yard chasing Chubby and then trying to wrangle that pork club out of his little gator chompers. It's a whole-ton easier to close one of those critters' mouths than it is to open one.

"We could just cook the whole gator!" Andy slurred. Miriam slapped the shit out the back of his head and he threw up a good stream again. Me and Pete were holding Chubby by his legs and his belly I don't know how exactly. We just had him grabbed one way or another when Pete toked up a smoke and blew a paper-mill's worth of happy into that gators snout. That gator toddler looked straight in Pete's eyes and grinned like I doubt I'll ever see again, then he sucked that whole goddam pork club down in one slurp, plastic and all.

"He made that pork stick disappear."

"Goddam. That was a hell of a case of the munchies." Andy was laughing and slinging spit off his hand after wiping his face. "You guess that's what Lazarus got?"

Miriam slapped him again.

27

I called home to check on my boys. Momma said they still had a freezer full of Hot Pockets and a stack of videotapes. Said the boys were fine, could barely even pick up their bottom jaws at this point for all the mouth breathing and video watching. I was happy with that and picked up Miriam's bottle of Carlo from the table. I realized I loved that fancy taste near as much as she did. Turned the whole world purple.

Chubby had done what he done with our pork stick, so we pooled some money for a couple jars of pickles and a super pack of hot dogs. People were going to start showing again and they'd be hungry. Folks got fed at a person's wake, and they'd be expecting to get something in their bellies. I volunteered to walk down to the Tiger Mart and everybody liked that idea because they knew I'd bring back their change if there was any. The same couldn't be said for some in that room. I hadn't managed to pick up any of the more expensive habits that sometimes came with growing up in the park.

Zach was working the Mart and we jabbered-on for a second. He'd gotten the day off to watch Jeffers big trick. Watched the whole thing from a tree but said he couldn't see real good for some of the branches in his way. I told him what I could, but I was even start-ing to doubt the details. He told me he was sorry anyhow, 'cause he knew that me and Jeffers were basically brothers. I'd never really spent much time with Zach except for buying beer and hotdogs and chips. People had told me he'd settled down a lot from a bad trip, and I told him to come on by if he got the chance. We'd be drinking all night again for sure.

I rounded everything up and got me a big beer for my troubles, took a breather, and walked to the river before heading back over to Miriam's place. The river was peeking through the last little bit of woods and I peeked back. The little white seabirds with the skinny bills were hanging out in the marsh grass in six-packs being lazy and looking like twigs themselves. Power lines stretched out for miles. I was wondering how they got that way and feeling a little more than drunk. Folks were fishing under bridges. All those half-trees and pick-up trucks, palm scrub and fart marsh, shell beds and meth heads all mashed up and flattened to the water. Birds rode the breezes and ducks dove. The big water flowed backwards, and I walked out to the dock.

Jeffers and me had been walking out on the same crumbling dock since we were kids. I didn't even know whose it was. The house burned down a long time ago and nobody bothered to rebuild. Probably were dead or just didn't have the money. We'd fished off that dock and seen every kind of animal imaginable. Some big ass sea cow started making fart noises at me and blow-ing bubbles. I guess he was just breathing, but he sure had a funny way of doing it. These things were so friendly. I was kinda wanting to just hang with him. He came back up, turned on his back, and I poured some of my beer in his mouth. He gurgled a little, but

I think he liked it and I gave him a couple pickles. He didn't jive with those and started mooing like they do.

"Man, you got a good deal don't you?" I poured him a little more beer in his mouth. "I swear I'd join you if I had my float." I was sitting down now, legs hanging off the slick rotten wood. "You ought to come to the races. You might fit in a van."

That manatee gurgled and blew more bubbles, lying there on his back. He'd polished off about half my beer and kept grunting for more. I finished it off real quick.

"I figure I better get on." He just lay there.

The river was looking like god's own lover dropped a mirror from her tramping purse. He got to see purple clouds and the pale pink sky from above. Every now and then a pretty good view on a reflection of us folks down there and remembered we were still around and would toss a whole cigarette on the ground for me to get to pick up and smoke for a minute, maybe a little longer. He'd throw some animal shapes in those shadow puppet clouds and the streetlights that never quite turned off all the way to stop struggling against morning would just keep on haunting until twilight. The top of the water shimmied just enough to make the reflection not quite right and gave the world above the reminder that things weren't perfect. I got up and shook my legs, trying to get them to come back to life—started walking.

When I looked back, I saw that sea cow spinning barrel rolls. I walked up the dock back to the grassy bank. Sonsabitches can't hold their liquor, but they're pretty good listeners.

I made it back to Miriam's place, giving the hotdogs a sniff to make sure they were still good after cooking in the sun for a bit.

Miriam was on the front porch. I could hear music coming from inside, just a steady thump of some turbo-charged, line-dancing bass.

"Where you been?" She was pretty in the sunlight. I could see why Jeffers took to her. All shoulder length brown hair, fair skin, big straight front teeth with chips to keep them interesting.

"Had a beer with a manatee."

"One of the mermaids? Where'd you see them at?"

"Nah. One in the river."

"Oh. They sure are the best, aren't they?" She was genuine. "Can't really handle much, though."

"Sure enough." I walked up the steps and handed her the bag of stuff.

"People are already showing back up."

Miriam wasn't fooling around. There were probably twenty people that had come in since I was gone. They must've walked, 'cause I didn't see any more cars out front. Zach had somehow beat me there. No wonder Miriam was thinking about what happened to me. He brought a couple suitcases of diet Bud and I snagged one out of the fridge to get my buzz working again. I busted out the pickles on the table and folks started walking around gnawing on them. Chubby tap-danced around looking up at the neon-green pickles in people's hands, mouth hanging open, and he reminded me of Lazarus on the sign out front of the Alligator Zoo-Park. He was just waiting on somebody to drop a pickle in. I imagined Mr. Cotter'd probably have to be taking that sign down now that Jeffers dropped in.

Knock Knock Knock

The only two people that ever knocked on Miriam's front door was Jeffers and Hecho.

Me and Miriam looked at each other, then turned around real quick. I got up from the floor where I'd been tasked with fixing the coffee table from the night before, which meant sorting through the pieces of pulpwood and trying to glue them together with some Elmer's.

I walked over to the door, slapping my hands together and trying to rub the glue off my fingertips. The door was already hanging open, spring busted, and flapping against the delaminated aluminum. I looked out both ways and nobody was on the stoop, so I pulled the door shut and turned around to the kitchen. Hecho was standing in there with a fish tank full of horchata and a steaming tinfoil ball of what smelled like tamales. He set the fish tank down and held up the tinfoil.

"Momma made 'em."

Don't know how that speedy bastard snuck in. This was the first I'd seen him since last track night. But I was happy to see him as ever. I'd heard he had a good time with the sheriff.

In about two seconds, I was eating my second tamale. Hecho was telling me about how many beers he and Chuck had managed to drink and still not shoot each other. They didn't miss a bottle.

The thought reminded me I was parched and needed another something to wash down the tamales. I was trying to make one but coming across some mixings was harder than I imagined. There was a plastic bottle of rum and some orange juice in the fridge. I poured it all in a glass and called it done, took a one-hitter over to the couch and dumped myself on it upside down for a few puffs.

With my drink on the patched up coffee table, life hit pause, slowed, stopped. The ball bounced on the screen for some word I couldn't read upside down. At that point I probably wouldn't have been able to read it right side up. I started to feel my face melt again. I'm not even sure I could move it. I just hung there like a goddam bat and let it go numb. It was funny watching the smoke blow out of my nose and mouth, head down and get lost, only to go back up. I guess smoke just wasn't meant to sink. Jeffers got him a real big breath before he went down. He could only stay down so long.

28

The afternoon was losing its burnt orange glow and the sun was trying to hide behind what was left of the fence. My eyes got blurry, and the line between day and night got thinner. Halos floated on nearly everything. I started thinking I was seeing people's ghosts. They were purple and blue, yellow and strange. Miriam's house was feeling a little haunted. I was probably looking more-than-creepy watching all these people and their trails walking around. When I tried to shake it off, my mouth let a little string of spit fly out the sides. I wiped it off the counter with my shirtsleeve. Tammy had been hanging around. She looked over at me all curious and such. I pointed to the bottom of my can, then walked over to the fridge to find me a couple Bud Lights, help get my head right, but there was nothing left. It was empty except for a bottle of ketchup and somebody's shoe on the top shelf. Miriam had her a Culligan water cooler she stole from the Alligator Zoo-Park employee lounge. It was empty too, but there were a bunch of big jugs on the floor. I thought I'd be nice, make up for some of my transgressing, and went on and spilled water all over the place putting that new one up on there. Course, I slipped trying to walk away. Miriam kept her cigarettes stashed next to the door and I grabbed me a smoke. Miriam walked back in, rubbing her sore knees and looking a wreck.

"Jimmy, can you grab me the new bag of cat food out from the back of the van?" Miriam was pushing Chubby around with her foot, trying to keep him away from a string-cheese she was working on. His mouth was hanging open and his eyes were all big and crazy. He'd followed her from the time she walked through the door.

"How many times a day you feed him?"

"Too many." She pushed him pretty good and he slid over toward the door on his belly. "A bunch more when he's been smoking like he has."

"I swear he's looking bigger than when I got here."

"It was that meat stick he got a hold of. I swear it's like miracle grow when he gets one of them." Toddler-gator was already tapping back over toward her ankles. "I left the cat food in the van. He gets a little spoiled from me being lazy."

She was still being lazy, but I could see she wanted to wash up. She handed me the keys, and I didn't mind. I needed some air and took the long way around, a little extra mileage to the side where her van was parked. The air outside had leveled off and was starting to break in the late afternoon.

I jingled the keys to try and keep steady, walked leg-across-leg over through the tall grass. I kept a hand on the fence, not caring much for the splinters, and let my fingers bump along till I could put a hand on her van there on the side of the house. The whole world was feeling a little melty. After about the fifth try, I got the tailgate to lift, and found the bag of cat food—some off-brand number that Miriam probably imagined Chubby wouldn't care much about. Had some black-and-white cat looking bored as all hell, just wanting somebody to give it some milk instead of a glamor shot. The bag stressed "value" and was sitting on top of cut-off notices for the power and a clipped-out ad for a beauty school up in Jacksonville. She was always dreaming big. I grabbed her mail and the food and started around for the front of the house. A little breeze kicked up and I got to see some moss dangle in the trees. I watched that until I got the spins. The asphalt smelled like mildew and I knew the rain would come back. It was on a schedule.

The air was cooler than I remembered from earlier and the breeze blew through my shirt. Got my nips all hard. I got up the steps, one at a time, and slumped over the front porch railing, let my head rest in my hands. Let myself feel something. When I closed my eyes I saw green and purple and electric streaks of light and things got to spinning again and made me get a little sick feeling. It wouldn't be long before I'd be needing another drink all sorts of critical. Couldn't sober up like this, it'd be real bad. Started trying to breathe through my nose and let some air in my brain, kept my eyes on the level. When they stopped moving, I noticed somebody had parked in Jeffers' ruts that he'd always let the NAILR mellow into. They'd been empty for a couple days, kinda out of reverence. Some sonofabitch didn't know and they'd humped their van up in the yard right in his spot on the same blotch of antifreeze the neighborhood cats were always sipping on. I started feeling heated and forgetful 'bout my drunk self. When I stepped off the porch, must've jumped four stairs at once, and got down to one knee in the grass. Pulled myself up and had it in my mind to key the holy hell out of that van.

Problem was, that van looked just like Jeffers' van. Had the NAILR car tag on it and all. Some kinda joke for somebody to be pulling a dead man's car up in the yard like that and leaving it. But it looked fresher than the NAILR. Like the NAILR got all her dings popped-out and a fresh set of tires, maybe even a new coat of paint. I put my hands on the hood and stood there straining my eyes, looking real deep down through the windshield, riding empty waves until I could feel the heat pulse through my fingertips and realized it was hot enough for them to sizzle.

I stumbled back up to the house, totally disbelieving and half-wondering if Jeffers could've followed through on something so simple and totally impossible as cheating death. When I got inside everybody else was figuring out the booze was gone, but nobody was signing up to get more. They were grabbing shirts and shoes and such, but I was looking around for somebody specific. I pushed people out of the way looking around for folks taller than me. There were a few of those, for sure. I was ignoring folks one at a time and generally just not concerning myself with their getting pissy when I pushed them. Tina was beer-whistling through another round of channeling David Allan Coe with no back-up when I caught her with one of my elbows, near knocking another tooth out. I turned off the karaoke machine.

"Hey!" I yelled, and the room stopped maybe for a second. "Y'all hold up!" They looked my way, some of them, but they knew I might've had a couple and got back to packing it up. Folks were moving slower and faster and slower again. The walls all felt orange from lamplight and the heat from the glow of a bunch of bodies. Don't know how people were standing up anymore when they looked so soft and runny. I think I tried to yell again, but don't know that a sound came out.

I gave up, searched around room-by-room, but no Jeffers. A couple folks were getting heated in the back bedroom, and a couple of them snorting on stuff in the bathroom. Somebody was going through Miriam's dresser drawers in her room. But all that didn't have me caring too much. Just me looking for a ghost and floating along just like one. I got to wondering if maybe he was invisible, might start playing jokes on folks like I knew for sure most ghosts did. Back in the den, I looked over the crowd again. Not sure any of those folks even knew what he would've looked like. I didn't know who some of those folks were, and definitely couldn't have called them by name. The room cleared, they funneled right on out the front door like the tap was left open. I was watching heads while they disappeared one after another and didn't see the one that mattered. The front door closed and the room was empty. The fridge vibrated all angry 'cause it got left open. The draft blew, but I couldn't feel it from where I stood, just saw a picture Miriam had taped to the wall flittering a little in the cool breeze.

I walked to the sliding door and it was still cracked, probably from me stumbling through before. The yard was dark from the back deck. Just a black hole except for the fire hole getting started and the flames scraping at the fresh night sky. I could see the shapes and shadows of the last few folks. They were the same ones that started this thing off. Pete and Andy and Tommy, for sure, all huddling around Miriam's chair with somebody sitting on the arm.

"You alright, Jimmy?" Somebody was asking from the fire hole. I wasn't sure. I couldn't come up with a good answer 'cause I didn't know how to tell a soul about what I saw out there in the front of the house.

"I guess." I was floating out toward the fire now. Drifting like smoke and realizing I left my cigarette on the front railing. Probably burned up by then. Didn't get who was asking me about myself.

"It's always, 'I guess.' When're you going to just be alright?"

It all sounded familiar and comforting. Familiar as my favorite glass, the smell of a car after a few hundred thousand miles, a pet's whine, or a creaky door. The smell of an Arctic Ice air freshener hanging from a rearview, or the cracking noise a beer made. Like I could put my head on a pillow and be in a dream, backing me up a few days to a time that felt smooth like fro-yo on a summer day.

Jeffers was sitting on the arm of Miriam's chair. He was looking just about as clean and comfortable as could be. He lost his beard. Looked maybe like he got him a haircut too. Tommy was standing there poking at Jeffers' arm and checking out a row of teeth marks looking like zig-zags, saying things like, "Holy shit."

I clenched my mouth real tight sucked my lips in to a curl, let my eyes get watery. I sniffed deep and held onto that breath about as long as I could, maybe a few seconds. Then I got to blubbering. Really felt like I was letting about thirty years and three-days-worth of bummed-out flow there down my face.

"We runned—we're all out of booze." I was sobbing. My chest was moving out of my control and I didn't even get to have a beer in my hand to feel comfortable. Jeffers stood up and put his arm around my shoulder.

"Nah, Jimmy. It's inside, right there in front of you."

I started rambling in my head, all the way from the beginning, back when me and Jeffers were just babies with nobody giving two shits about us being around or alive or what have you. How we learned magic because it made us better than dirt. How he left me behind but was always there somehow to leave me behind again, but that he hadn't really ever left me. I got to feeling dangerously close to reality. Went riding on that tilt-a-whirl of feeling a little displeased about not getting to see Jeffers first. In fact, I was the last of them that got to see him. I'd gotten left out of the last trick and left out of the big finale. On top of that, I had about a billion-and-a-half questions. Jeffers walked me over to the water cooler and poured me a big cup. I didn't get it. I didn't want water. That stupid cooler did its glug-glug-glug and I needed something better. I near blew like a dolphin-hole when I sucked down that first sip and I let my questions and frustrations go elsewhere.

"That's shine!"

We never left the party, but Jeffers was gone by morning.

29

The wood slats in front of my face weren't letting any light through and my shorts were wet. I started pounding on the boards.

"Hello!

I was pounding harder now, knocking as hard as I could, but those boards were too close to my face. There was light around me somehow, and every time I moved my legs, trying to kick those boards, my thighs sloshed around in some kinda puddle.

"Hayyyy!"

Don't know how I got to being down there, but it sure enough freaked me out plenty.

"Jimmy! What the hell is your problem?" There was Miriam's head hanging down, for sure not hanging right side up. Had to turn my head to see her.

"Miriam! How'd you get down here?" I moved my leg again and realized Chubby had my shorts in his mouth.

"You're under my goddam bed, Jimmy."

Chubby was hanging heavy on my leg, snoozing a little closer to my business than I thought was right. That gator had been hanging onto my shorts like a lovey, drooling all over my shortpants. He was out cold.

"For sure ain't your squeaky toy, Chubby." I got to trying to move and that gator wasn't letting me loose. He grunted a little and pulled on my Umbros a little tighter. Couldn't have been less fabric between meat and teeth. I started slipping out of them. Had to leave my shorts down there with him. I got up and pulled my robe a little tighter.

"Where's Jeffers?"

Miriam was still wrapped up tight in the covers, looked like she got touched by every wheel of a semi.

"Gone when I woke up. Kinda thought you might know—might've talked to him."

"I was thinking I was in the ground, for sure."

"You staying for breakfast? Think I got some pickles or something out there." It was a half-assed offer, but I appreciated it. She didn't have to throw it out there. I was feeling numb in the teeth, some kinda weird pressure like my teeth might pop out of my head any second. Pickles weren't sounding right. Chubby was up and out from under the bed, went walking by with my Umbros hanging from his teeth like a prize. Stopped in the doorway and started rubbing his face in them. Can't imagine they smelled alright, hadn't showered in days, but he was into it, and I was a little flattered. I turned to make sure Miriam was seeing him. She was sitting up, covers not hiding much.

"He likes you, Jimmy."

"No shit."

I walked out the front door into a whole bunch of crazy. The morning paper was sitting there soggy on the steps, so I snatched it up. When I looked up I saw that the NAILR was gone. Instead, that same news van with the camera was humping and shaking down the road, moving all slow like it was hiding and waiting behind some bushes. I boogied on out of there before they could catch me in my undies again and jumped in the brush, started blazing a trail to find Jeffers. When I got to the road on the other side the sun was full-on showing up on the river. I spent some mornings watching boats cruise the channel and off to the side, the flats, dodging crab traps without so much as looking. Today I had a mission, so I sat down on the bank to do some thinking and read the paper. The board I sat down on was damp wood and felt it through my robe. I pulled the paper from the plastic bag and rolled it out. It was from four days ago and on one of those thin weekday papers with not a whole lot of comics. The headline was a big one, though. I had already seen it before.

Jeffers The Magnificent!

The picture was a cartoon of an alligator head popping out of a magic hat. Cartoon Jeffers looked funny, made his eyes all big and his features look a little whacked out. The assistant in the picture was a big-tittied woman. That for sure wasn't right, but they did have it right that it wasn't me anymore.

All the details were there, like it was telling the future, reading it right off my palms while I was holding the paper. Lots of words on the pages. It talked about his feeding the crowd chicken wings. How it wasn't what folks were wanting to see. How this was Jeffers' time for redemption. He was going to be pulling out all the stops. Folks never realized he was doing tricks all the time. That they weren't tricks at all. Always looking for answers and a gimmick, asking Jeffers to do it again. Jeffers'd always say, "You got eyes? Can't you see? It's right in front of you." But I was thinking everybody was blind as could be. Not so sure I wasn't blind my ownself. Stayed close and just kept on watching.

According to the paper, *The Times-Union* had been out to do a little investigative reporting, checking out the springs, making sure nothing was rigged up before Jeffers went on. There were going to be a whole lot of people, it said, a big crowd. The biggest Jeffers'd ever had around for sure. The gators were chattering and yapping, just laying around waiting on Jeffers and his big trick. It would be a NASCAR crowd. They were all going out there to see blood.

I watched the dredge and the fishing boats, sunshine bouncing bright spots off the water between breaks in the clouds. There was white on the tips of the water, the breeze was thirsty and lapped up the chop. Somebody was making the channel deeper, trying to bring more boats and more people, taking the muddy bottom and dumping it somewhere else. They would swallow us up from every side. I was getting squeezed out from every comfortable spot in my world, pretty soon I'd be in some other nowhere. I left the river how it was and drifted to where I was thinking Jeffers would be, the Alligator Zoo-Park.

The sign out front said:

LIVE GATOR SHOWS

2X DAILY

R.I.P. JEFFERS

I walked through the employee gate 'cause it was open and smelled everything familiar. Not a soul was around, but the baby gators were sounding like Star Trek with all their ray-gun sounds, back-and-forth calling for momma. Some of the biggies were hissing and grumbling 'cause they were hungry while the others were sounding like motorboats from being lovesick. I was wondering if they'd been fed in a few days. They were restless. I felt spooked but for sure didn't feel alone. A thousand little eyes were looking at me telling me I was the wrong man, and I knew Jeffers wasn't there but kept looking anyhow.

When I got close to the main den, past the gift shop, and was about to walk right on by the mermaid tank, maybe get me a free coke from the stand, I saw what had the gators feeling odd.

Grown-ass man was sitting at the bottom of the mermaid tank, sucking on the air tube. Two big old gators were floating around the top, just circling and watching. The algae made it tough to see in. I got right up on the tank and in the green I saw Judd. Eyes open but in a galaxy of his own. He looked right back at me and I felt like I was seeing through a telescope. Judd was a planet and the gators circled like moons, ready to pull him back to the top. I couldn't save him, and he didn't want saving. I sat on the front row bench and looked for him to motion or try to say something, but it didn't look like he was wanting for much. Looked peaceful as could be. The otters and turtles weren't having any of it. They were nowhere to be seen. I left too.

I kicked the dirt and shook it off as I walked. It was still morning as far as I could tell, and there was one more place Jeffers might be. The birds were preaching down at me from the trees and I swear the squirrels threw small branches, pinecones, and acorns.

Some hit me and some fell in the path ahead of me. The locusts in the trees got rolling and timed to my steps. A fly buzzed in my open mouth and caught in my throat. I coughed until it flew out like it had just gone in there out of curiosity. I walked through the woods until I found the street. I passed the stain on the ground, a mixture of blood and beer from the deer that took out my van and got a fresh dose of life. He was still out there living, maybe enjoying things he took for granted before. The yellow sign of the Waffle House even glowed in the daytime—a beacon for the weary. The NAILR was parked right out front.

"Welcome to the Waffle House!" like they'd never seen me before.

Jeffers was sitting in a booth with Teri hunched over the table showing him how her wrist was hurt. Flopping it back-and-forth and breathing through her teeth.

"I think I got the carpal tunnels. I need healing." She had the saddest look on her face. Looked even sadder when she saw me walk up, gave me the once over.

"It hurt when you're moving it?" Jeffers caught a look of me sitting down. "Jimmy!"

Teri still stood there, wiggling her wrist.

"Only when I'm working," she said.

"I'll take a coffee."

Teri frowned at me but realized that her time was probably up.

"Jimmy, you're looking like a mess." I didn't notice the folks all turned around looking at me, till he said something. Kind of wished he wouldn't have. I pulled my robe a little tighter, made sure the knot was tight.

"Why'd you take off this morning?"

"You were snoring under the bed." That didn't really do much for people paying less attention to my getup. "Went and saw Aunt Becky."

"Man, I thought you were dead."

Teri dropped my coffee on the table, spilled a little. I wiped it up with the belt of my bathrobe, still looking at Jeffers so he couldn't disappear.

"Everybody did." Jeffers had him a bite of patty melt. Made me jealous. "Maybe I was. I told you I'd be back, though."

"That's not fair. Known you my whole life. We're supposed to tell our tricks."

"Who's saying it was a trick, Jimmy?"

"Lemme see your arm."

Jeffers held out his arm. The lines of teeth marks were red with silver-skin around them.

"Need to see more?"

I shook my head. Jeffers pulled up his shirt, anyhow. Had rows of marks like a constellation. Plain as day.

"How're you here?" The fog of a few days, maybe a lifetime, lifted.

"I never left you. Can't help that you still don't see what's right in front of you. Go home to your boys, Jimmy. Get some sleep."

I felt like I was sleep-walking out of there. Jeffers called after me when I got to the door.

"I'll pick you up for track night."

30

I walked over to the dog track to talk to Aunt Becky. Knew I'd find her there. A block or so later I was walking through the back lot of the track. It was a dirt lot, nice and shady, covered by big, old oak trees. The lot looked like it moved 'cause of the shadows from the wagging moss and the swaying trees. There were chicks and dudes making out in trucks. Everybody just kinda hung around and listened to the dogs barking and chattering in the kennels. Every now and then, a cop would come around and check on everybody and take in a beer with the kids while they talked about where they used to park. It was a friendly kind of place.

The pink and teal signs made the ground glow like the future. I walked through the lot, stopping for a second before the handicap spots and again before walking through the drop-off lane. These were both spots where I'd nearly been run-down by old ladies in previous visits. I grabbed the black handle of the glass double doors and felt how a room with good-working A/C should when I opened them.

Aunt Becky's spot was at the far table, tucked off to the side. I hung around her chair and held her place at the table while she squeezed one out and re-bought chips. It was the most she'd ever asked me to do besides get out of her house. When she came back she was on the button. She tipped the dealer for saving her spot but didn't thank me. Some old cooter was pissed and acting like he owned the table.

"I don't think she should get to be on the button if she wasn't even here for the deal. She's got to miss a round!" He sure enough didn't know who Aunt Becky was. She tipped dealers well and the bouncers better. She knew how to drink a string of gin and tonics and still get to spend the whole day at her table without dealing with a hound dog like that.

Toby wore about three hundred pounds on himself. He also wore a black shirt with a greyhound running full sprint in prison stripes stamped on the back of it and "Security" plain as day on the front. That poor old man stopped bitching 'cause he got dragged out by his throat.

Aunt Becky got her cards.

"Aunt Becky, I know you seen Jeffers." It wasn't the best time to ask her deep stuff, but it was hard to catch her any other time.

"Where're your pants?" She paused for a few, then kept on. "And why're you here while I'm working?" She tossed a couple chips in the pot. "Bet."

"I've got to know about Jeffers."

She tapped the table in front of the button. "Jeffers is Jeffers."

"What do you mean?"

"Bet." She pushed a small stack in to the middle of the table. "He's always been something else. Guess he'll be magic to the end. You boys known each other a long time. Think about it."

The waitress brought my drink and I handed her a few wadded-up dollars in the hopes it seemed like a bunch of money. She was sexy as hell. Real crazy blonde and perky, but super bitchy. I took a sip and it tasted like water. No respect.

"Bet." She pushed in a whole hell-of-a-lot of her chips and it made my knees a little shaky thinking about my shitty van and my trailer, me eating grilled cheese twice a day with my mouth all broken out in the creases while my boys go to a shitty school. Denny searching the bottom of an empty Reese's bag and Momma tongue deep in a bottle. Pete and Andy icing bruised knuckles and Tommy searching for proof of something better. Miriam waiting on the trick to end and Jeffers—Jeffers always escaping.

"Fold."

"Fold."

"Fold. Show them cards, woman." Some dude wanted to test her after he'd already given her all the respect she needed to take his money.

"Hell no." She slid her cards to the dealer and stacked her chips all tidy and that dude didn't ask again.

"So, you're saying this is it? He's done become a new Jeffers and that's all fine and done?"

"I'm saying, Jeffers has always been this Jeffers." She was annoyed as hell. Turned around to look at me, like she needed to spell it for me. "He's left you before, he'll be gone again. He's high-flying." Made her hands into a bird and turned right back around. "Question is: why are you still here?"

I sucked my drink down through the two little straws and watched the room for a second. Then turned to leave.

"Aunt Becky."

"Uh-huh."

"Thanks—for."

Aunt Becky grabbed my arm and took my hand, put a chip in my hand and wrapped my fingers around it.

"Give this to Toby on the way out, would you? For getting that old asshole out of here."

"Yes, ma'am." I was waiting for something and it took a second for the words to settle, after what I thought was water competed for mental space.

I handed the chip to Toby on the way out and he looked like he wanted to kill me.

"From Aunt Becky."

He just kind of looked. I'm not sure he knew what was going on. He just wanted to kill a rabbit like some oversized pup. Should've put his ass on the track and run him a little bit.

I stopped in the Tiger Mart on the way home, needing to settle my stomach a little and get my head right. I picked up a couple grape Swishers and a six-pack of Bud, a pack of Oberto and the last hot dog from the rollers. It was more money than I should have dropped. Beef jerky is a treat and I knew I should have just grabbed a can of Vienna sausages, but I was feeling unsettled. I could justify the coin as long as the kids got a bite or two. I took a stack of napkins from the dispenser to get my money's worth.

By the time I got to the house, I still had four beers left and I wrapped up a couple of bites of the hot dog in a napkin and stuck it on the counter. The bag of Jerky was empty. I did my best to stick it down in one of my cans so the boys wouldn't find it and feel neglected if they happened to sort their way through the trash looking for scrap. They wouldn't be home from school for a little while, so I cracked and shook the filling out of a Swisher. Thankfully, there were a few seeds and whatnot in my shoebox. I rolled-up the seeds in the grape wrapper and torched that sonofabitch.

When I stirred, a child was punching me in my left cheek, thanking me for the bite of hot dog. I felt like an asshole for how low I set the bar but couldn't be more pleased with his thankfulness. I gave him a big hug and wiped the charred remains of the Swisher off my shirt.

The skin of my lower back sucked off the couch when I stood up and took a second to let my eyes do their thing adjusting to the light leaking in from the broken-ass shades on the windows. I stepped on a string of ants all the way to the sliding back door and watched the palm fronds wag in the evening breeze. The river was still there a few blocks away and the snakes were still in the bushes. A squirrel chattered loud enough to hear through the glass and the crickets were getting their party started in the tall grass. I wondered what they liked instead of beer and if they drank it all night like I did.

Whack.

"Goddamit." I was having a peaceful moment. One of the kids tried to take out my knees with that Flintstone's bat. I snatched it up and issued a blanket warning to both of them, even though the other one wasn't in the room. The clock on the VCR was flashing 6:40, telling me that Jeffers didn't pick me up.

"Jeffers come by?"

"Nope!"

I took the bat with me to the bathroom and closed the door,

showed my teeth to myself in the mirror and they looked alright. Jeffers and I had known each other for near-every single one of our thirty some-odd years. We always rode together to track night. He knew my van only started sometimes. We drank so many beers that we could've filled the river with the empties. Now he wasn't even going to pick me up. I had to get out to the track by seven, so I got out into the yard to start dicking around with the van. The mosquitos found my legs, even hidden under my jeans. The sonsabitches were just as hungry as I was. I rattled the Flintstone's bat against the side of the van as I walked up to chase the blue tailed skinks and any other critters out from under it. I only saw two skinks, so I felt somewhat safe popping the hood and sticking my nose down in there.

The battery terminals were caked with corrosion. It looked like little piles of rock candy and I thought about sticking my tongue on one of them to see if there was still some kick. Sweat puddled in my eyes and I feared a tear might have snuck in there. I thought back to the first time we ran our vans off the line. We pooled our cigarettes and some cash to enter the races. This was back when my wheels ran and his didn't. I would pick Jeffers up and we'd get real stoned to settle our nerves. Shit, he got me turned on to the grape blend. We cooled off with beer and filled our guts with pork rinds. I could barely hang on to the steering wheel it got to being so greasy.

I felt a little sick from all my reminiscing. Maybe it was the thought of the pork rinds. I dropped the wire leads of the battery and leaned over, hurling a smidge in the bushes.

"Jimmy, what the hell you doing?" It was Momma. She'd always been trying to give me a heart attack.

"Just thinking, Momma. Why're you going to sneak up on a man like that?"

"I'm picking up the boys. You just thinking your brains out in the bushes?"

I rolled up to the track an easy hour later, dazed more than a little on sentimentality and intoxicants. Jeffers was already there. He'd won his first heat and was sucking on a coke can. Maybe he was dipping.

"Hey Jimmy, how you?" It was something like that. It was generic, but he still called me Jimmy. He didn't give me any shit for being late, for missing his first run, but he'd also been the one to not pick me up. There was already jabbering in the crowd that he'd broken a record. I didn't ask. I just wanted to be around, to talk, to hear him speak, to see another miracle. We all got spoiled. He was a drug, but beyond any of that bathtub shit that they cooked up down the block. He was the real deal and it seemed like everyone was stopping by to have a snort or a huff. We sat on the bumper of NAILR.

"You got beers?"

"I'm drinking Captain in the can here."

"Good stuff."

"Feeling like taking flight."

"That good?"

"I'm higher than you can imagine."

"Why're you leaving me out like that?"

"Like what?"

"Like you just said. You keep cutting me out. This was *our* thing." I was pushing it, trying to be dramatic as hell. I didn't really feel all that bad. I just wanted him to think about me while he was out there floating.

"Still is. Don't think twice about it. Somebody's got to carry on, though. You're the man to do it. I'm barely a man anymore."

I snorted. "You a woman now?" But he was looking out beyond me. I put my chin over my shoulder where I thought he was staring, but there wasn't a damn thing over there. When I turned back he was walking around to the driver's side door. I reckoned it was time for his next heat.

"Jimmy, I'm about to burn up the streets. No records left for me here."

"Whatever, man. Do it. Good luck."

"Just know it's for real."

I knew he'd make those wheels spin like videotape, fast-forwarding through thirty years.

"Yeah, you too."

Jeffers cranked the NAILR. I swear it was ready to take off. No rattling, no shaking, just firing like some phantom space ship ready to warp and blur in front of my eyeballs. I walked over to Miriam. She had been sitting there on a bench up against the old hangar. Her face was all scrunched up in her hands like a dog on a calendar that wanted me to pine over its cuteness for a whole month.

"What're you doing?"

"Nothing. Watching these fools race."

"Not nice to call somebody a fool."

"I feel like a fool. She pointed over at Jeffers. "I don't get him anymore."

"You're no fool."

Jeffers looked over at me and I swear he winked. Maybe he winked at Miriam, but she wasn't looking. I'm sure it was at me. He did that sort of thing sometimes. Just a nod or a shrug. Said something without having to talk. He squeezed the pedal down in neutral a couple times and the engine whinnied like the smallest of ponies on the steepest of inclines. He always waited till the last second to strap his helmet, and that's just what he did but in his own way. He was as unique a sonofabitch as ever been made or shot out a woman in a pig barn. But there he was tying a knot in the straps 'cause the clickers were missing. Jeffers squeezed that pedal one more massive time and the light went greenish. He dropped the shifter to OD and caught a little rubber before the NAILR fired on down the old runway.

But this time it really fired. Jeffers had ignored his mail, opting to live in the moment, and we found later that a dozen or so recall notices for a faulty gas tank vent were missed.

It wasn't so much of a boom as it was a suck-blow. The flames came out the tailpipe first like the goddamn bat mobile. The flame didn't go out, it went in, and the back end of the NAILR became a big ball of bright. I'm not even sure that he knew he'd jumped down into hell 'cause he was still flooring that thing. He was a shooting star leaving a tail like the flamingest comet I ever laid eyes on. But I'm pretty sure the only comet I ever saw before this one was in a book about space or something. He was a shooting star, a dancing sun on the runway. I swear he took off.

When the NAILR finally stopped, it was near the tall pines beyond the grass strip and way past the end of the runway. He made it across the field, like one final Hail Mary pass. And he left a strip of char all the way. That strip is still there, nothing grows 'cause he sucked all the life that could ever be lived out of it. Jeffers didn't leave the smallest piece of himself there in the van. He vanished. In the heat from the heap of melty metal I looked up and swear the sun started bouncing around the late-afternoon sky. Jeffers had knocked one final trick out of the park before he left for good. But that was the trick. He disappeared without a trace. Sure, they thought they found some teeth, but for real, that wasn't Jeffers. Those probably belonged to somebody else, maybe an animal. Jeffers wasn't an animal. He was a vapor and a flame, and liquid and just a drop of the ether.

ACKNOWLEDGEMENTS

Thank you to:
Elizabeth, Margaux, and Brer for absolutely everything.

For your friendship, mentorship, and guidance—Erica Dawson,
Jeff Parker, Jess Anthony, Kevin Moffett, Robert Olmstead,
Jason Ockert, and Fiona McCrae

For your support, friendship, generosity, hospitality, and/or patience—
Jared Rypkema, Caleb Sarvis, and the Bridge Eight team.

Riley Manning, Grace Lanoue, and Michael Weber, Hank & Jan, Mom &
Dad, Carson, David, Jensen Beach, Shane Hinton, Harrison Scott Key,
Ty Williams, Josh Giles, Matthew Logan Vasquez, Justin Hall

The magic, the people, and the program of DISQUIET

The entire University of Tampa family and Lynne Bartis for posting bail

The alligators of the Hillsborough for not being that hungry

Sean George for introducing me to Hot Fries

Ms. O'Connor and Mr. Crews, Ms. Hurston
and Ms. Rawlings for cutting a path

The Hub, The Retreat, Flask & Cannon, Poe's, Pete's, and Maria Caxuxa

The communities of South Georgia and Florida that I've called home

Jacksonville and Florida, for staying wild and wonderful

"C.H. HOOKS IS A DAMNED WIZARD, AND ALLIGATOR ZOO-PARK MAGIC IS A HOLY HELL OF A BOOK."

- Harrison Scott Key, author of *Congratulations, Who Are You Again?* and *The World's Largest Man*

Is Jeffers an Alligator Zoo-Park magician or the Messiah? Two friends live unapologetically on the edge of poverty in the rugged, un-decorous part of the South. Jimmy, a single father with an addict ex, and Jeffers, a magician whose tricks are closer to miracles—both are immersed in a place where trailers and Hot Pockets dominate the landscape, and alligators roam free. When Jimmy witnesses "losing" his best friend to his biggest trick gone awry, he reflects on their lifelong friendship and what it really means to escape.

"DRAW A DIRECT LINE FROM LARRY BROWN AND HARRY CREWS TO C.H. HOOKS."

- Jeff Parker, author of *Ovenman*

"MR. HOOKS HAS PRODUCED A MAGIC SHOW OF THE HIGHEST ORDER."

- Jensen Beach, author of *Swallowed by the Cold*

"ALLIGATOR ZOO-PARK MAGIC IS IN THE BEST TRADITION OF SOUTHERN LITERATURE — IT'S FAST AND FUNNY, DARK AND DESPERATE."

- Shane Hinton, author of *Pinkies* and editor of *We Can't Help It If We're From Florida*

C.H. Hooks writes and lives with his family in Brunswick, GA. He received an MFA from the University of Tampa and is a Lecturer at the College of Coastal Georgia. This is his debut novel.

www.chhooks.com
Instagram: @chhooks
Twitter: @ch_hooks

BRIDGE EIGHT PRESS
www.bridgeeight.com
@bridgeeightpress

Cover illustrations by Ty Williams
Cover design by Jared Rypkema & Cassie Deogracia
Author photograph by Miriam Berkley

$15.95
ISBN 978-1-7323667-1-8
51595

9 781732 366718